DEAD IN

LONG BEACH,

CALIFORNIA

DEAD IN
LONG BEACH,
CALIFORNIA

VENITA BLACKBURN

MCD
Farrar, Straus and Giroux
New York

MCD
Farrar, Straus and Giroux
120 Broadway, New York 10271

Library of Congress Cataloging-in-Publication Data
Names: Blackburn, Venita, author.
Title: Dead in Long Beach, California / Venita Blackburn.
Description: First edition. | New York : MCD / Farrar Straus and
    Giroux, 2024.
Identifiers: LCCN 2023030820 | ISBN 9780374602826 (hardback)
Subjects: LCGFT: Psychological fiction. | Novels.
Classification: LCC PS3602.L325289 D43 2024 | DDC 813/.6—
    dc23/eng/20230707
LC record available at https://lccn.loc.gov/2023030820

Our books may be purchased in bulk for promotional,
educational, or business use. Please contact your local
bookseller or the Macmillan Corporate and Premium Sales
Department at 1-800-221-7945, extension 5442, or by email at
MacmillanSpecialMarkets@macmillan.com.

www.mcdbooks.com • www.fsgbooks.com
Follow us on social media at @mcdbooks and @fsgbooks

10 9 8 7 6 5 4 3 2 1

To those who missed their goodbyes

FRIDAY

WE ARE RESPONSIBLE FOR TELLING THIS STORY, mostly because Coral cannot. She just discovered her brother dead in his apartment. Suicide. Coral's brother, Jay, lived in Long Beach, California. It was a cheap apartment even though he could afford more. Jay didn't like the idea of moving, because no one really likes the idea of moving, especially men nearing forty. People like to dream of being elsewhere and suddenly having all their things elsewhere with them, but moving is what Coral refers to as *some bullshit*. We've done the research. The apartment peeked out from between a row of houses and one other multiunit building. Bougainvillea, gardenias, and other low-water-tolerant plants that add pops of color to lazy landscaping crawled along the facing. Long Beach was an oily, salty city nicknamed Weirdbeach by those not likely to fly a gay pride flag on their lawns anytime soon. The long, sleepy horns of boats at the extremely active port moaned into the night. Coral had finished a brief conversation with Jay about eleven minutes before arriving at his apartment. He didn't mention the suicide. We are certain.

There wasn't much blood. There wasn't much blood visible right away, that is. We believe this is why Coral didn't notice when she walked in. The studio was dark, the way Jay liked it, with blue walls, a blue sofa, a blue entertainment center and blue rug. It was like diving into the ocean at any time of day, if the ocean were hot as fuck, humid, and smelled like burned bacon and coconut-scented candles. Coral thought the place was empty but was startled when she saw the shape of Jay under a blanket on his bed.

It was so quiet I thought no one was home, Coral said. She went to the kitchen and looked in the refrigerator.

You need to go to the grocery store. Where's the water? It's hot as fuck in here. Yeah, I was surprised when they offered me the deal, but now that it's signed I can talk about it, you know. I know you knew something was up and I don't keep people in suspense with hints and things, but it's like a pregnancy. You don't talk about that shit until it's deep in the process and you know for sure. That's what people say, at least. Men don't think about that junk. Let me give you another metaphor, since that is what I do. So it's like in football when you talk about who is going to win or not. You don't jinx that shit by oversharing why you know. Or maybe that is what you do. Y'all be extra with that down to the mathematical. Mofos walking around with 300 credit scores can recite every statistic from 1967 to the present about some team. How are you still under that blanket?

That's when Coral walked close to the body of Jay in the dim light and saw what we know. She handled it as well as could be expected, which is not well in the long run, not well at all. Some people scream at death. Coral fell down with vertigo. Everything silent. The heart causes that, pumps all the blood to all the extremities so it feels like your head is going to pop, and your fingertips go numb with the pressure. She tried to grip her phone and couldn't. She tried to breathe and couldn't. Failure to accomplish basic tasks is typical when in shock. Time moves differently. The body becomes lighter and heavier simultaneously, like dark matter. One goes in and out of existence involuntarily. We know it was three minutes before Coral came to her senses and called 911. The phrase *came to her senses* is a common one, so we used it, but it is spectacularly inaccurate. Losing the illusion of safety in this life is being more at one with the senses than ever. Glimpsing death does this. It is a reminder that people were tender, shell-less, watery husks of nerves. Because so much could hurt them, we believe that forgetting some pain was even possible allowed people to choose existence, to become numb to every sensation. There is no replacement for that kind of amnesia about mortality; the simulations in games or movies are not close. Death IRL is an ice bath from the inside out. Still, we like to think that in other circumstances, where an emergency was more time-sensitive, Coral would've behaved better, but we have our doubts and would not put money on that outcome.

Coral wrote us into existence. She made us and we made her money and brought her minor fame in exchange. We are students of her time, this time, and as students we practice what is known. In the Clinic for Excavating Repressed Memories in Search of Solutions to Current Crises, we are a child of approximately seven years. We are on a boat with our family, playing with a baby squid. We play with the squid as children do, with a reckless disregard for things like pain or worse. Everything in the sea then was young because everything ancient had been caught and consumed. The squid finally dies in our hands while we scantily notice. We do notice a white lump in the flesh and with a pair of tweezers in our mother's tool kit we grip the hard nub and pull. What emerges shocks and disgusts us, the core of the squid comes cleanly out, almost as long as our forearm, hollow as a bird's bone and sealed in what looks like a fin of translucent plastic: the pen. We are not at all certain what we expected to pull from the corpse in our hands, though we estimate it must have been something familiar to a human child of that age, a thing not grotesque in nature but a thing that possesses some great usefulness, like a pearl or a tooth, a pretty thing that can bite enemies or earn us praise if we hold it up in front of our little brother. But the internal shell is none of those things, neither pretty nor useful, and we drop our tweezers and the entire mess of the wrecked beast onto the deck at our feet. Then there comes the laughter. We forget that we are not alone on the boat, because we startle at the sound of our brother's voice. We know we startle easily, but certainly we had forgotten many things in that moment with the dead squid. We'd forgotten we were seven years old headed to Catalina Island with a confident but incompetent seafaring father, a bored mother and brother. Many years later we would be on that same boat as teenagers, our father and no mother, our brother seventeen, holding a portable Discman spinning a CD, Snoop Dogg's first album, the one with the naked woman's ass sticking out of a doghouse. We believe it to be his best album. But that was a decade to come. Then we were children and we began to cry.

Don't laugh at your sister.
Look at what she did.
What are you doing with that fish?

Our mother comes to us, the metal of her bracelets ringing as she picks up the squid and throws it over the side of the boat in disgust. She holds us by the shoulders and not so subtly wipes the squid juice on our sweater. Our brother laughs again.

We have measured the hormones, the chemicals of fright and disbelief, the boil of the blood when a person encounters the dead. As close to one being as all of humanity truly is and pretends to be in their poems and scriptures, there is something different when the dead is familiar, when the corpse is expected to be articulated with a remembered smell, sound, and texture. In the dead, those sounds are removed, the smell is vacated and replaced with something foreign yet instantly recognizable. Only those that have seen their beloveds expired know this space and none have named it well. We still do not give it letters or adequate pronunciation, but we catalog it with the rest of our fascinations along with celiac disease and mycelium. Coral would occupy that space in ways we did not predict and for a time we did not foresee. Jay's body formed a hill under the blanket, soft and dry at the feet, arching up to the stillness of his chest and shoulders, then descending to the catastrophe of his skull. The arm and hand holding the gun drooped gently. People spent their days in various shapes from the fleck of an embryo, eating, drinking, and swelling up into adulthood, and with a little luck and ingenuity arrived at old age. Everyone takes a final shape when they go to greet their gods, either sitting up watching television, or sometimes lying supine in hospice, or toes skimming the floor held up to the ceiling by the throat, or clutching a broom in a kitchen, or underneath a 1967 Corvette unscrewing the oil filter, or on the toilet in the throes of frustration, or with hands gripping a shopping cart in a grocery store, or watching the moon. Often luck and ingenuity were not enough to reach old age. Often.

Everyone was capable.

We created clinics to practice all the ways people stopped their lives in order for us to understand them better. The clinics look much like theaters designed to look like suburbs and farm communities and coastal villages and urban centers and abandoned cabins in dense unmapped woods. There were rooms for matricide, for sleeping pills, snake-bites, glass ingestion, broken hearts, swallowed tongues, roller-coaster decapitation, incidents in the shower (slips, stabbings, curtain asphyxiation), and the rest.

Humans evolved from primitive beings typically classified as hunter-gatherers. *Evolved* is a generous term because once the act of seeking out a desirable life-giving object and storing that life-giving object was imprinted into the DNA of the Species, there was no giving up the impulse. It survived from the moment a wise proto-woman saw a stack of berries and considered something so profound that it changed the behavior of her familial unit and all her progeny for millions of years. She saved those berries for Later. From that original action came boxes of various shapes and dimensions and with temperature controls for preservation of all life-giving objects discovered and plucked from the earth as well as from the imagination. Many ate well and at leisurely times, which had never happened before. Time prior to that was full of anxiety, overfull bellies, toothaches, and gastrointestinal variables, because eating and pleasure only existed in the present moment. There was no real concept of Later then, so everyone lived in a panic, devouring and fucking on urges that were not orderly. Fortunately, order did arrive, along with silos and refrigeration units and barrels and Tupperware and canning jars and ziplock bags. Later was commodified and sold in order to fill it with objects not yet needed but painstakingly arranged for. With the concept of Later came the perversion of More. Early humankind clearly had a keen sense of More. They always wanted More: more food, more water, more sex, more reasons to war for food, water, and sex. It wasn't complicated, but once Later entered their consciousness, the limits of More widened to hazardous extremes. Later had to be filled with More and Later, an abstract concept with no concrete parameters and that possessed a special range to hold endless junk and garbage or essential items that would eventually wither into junk and garbage. The perversion of More did not simply end with decay but also eroded the simple act of sharing. With limitless space in the future, there was little room left in the present to gauge how much was too much to keep for Later and to spare for others. And so humanity began to hoard. Oh, how they hoarded. Not just fruits of summer to last through a cold winter, but they hoarded everything, all the bits of detritus they could see and touch and fit into Later. They wanted More: more makeup, more comic books, money, allergy medicine, armies, court justices, cities, aqueducts, money, peanut butter, toilet paper, canning lids, duct tape, money, freeze-dried lasagna, blankets, and toy poodles. They took More and exploded themselves into panicked, depressed, fidgety, twitching things. They understood too late the solution to the perversion of more: Too Much. The notion of Too Much became law and culture and was taught to children in nursery rhymes and half-minute digital advertisements. Commerce was god and all prayed diligently. When they did discover the revolutionary idea of having too much, they had already taken too much to give back. Decay does not work backward in these instances.

The EMTs left the door of the apartment open as they worked. A rectangle of evening light lingered outside like a curious onlooker but never entered the dim living room. Jay was not a small man. Four EMTs hoisted him onto the stretcher. Coral watched like a supervisor. Her body became a spike, a cross, a tomb, an eye of God, a scepter, a thing to lay judgment on the face of anyone that failed to execute the tasks perfectly. Jay's phone dinged and vibrated like something hungry. Everyone turned to it, knowing what waited for the person that sent the message. The EMTs turned away, relieved that it was not their place. Coral picked up the phone. She expected to see the sender but not the entire message. Jay was one of the 28 percent of Americans that did not lock their phones.

Khadija: can't do dinner tonight daddy. Club is having a meeting. I'll text Coral too. Next Friday?

Coral swiped her finger up and the phone opened entirely.

Idiot, Coral said aloud.

We believe it is brave to not lock a phone. It's a declaration of self-sufficiency and the ability to hold on to one's secrets in tight fists and deep pockets. Coral believed it was the stupidest risk to take and the equivalent of walking around butt-ass naked while every stranger attempted to pinch a nipple and yank a pubic hair.

One of the EMTs spoke, instructions on what to do next, how police would arrive to talk to her shortly, and which facility the deceased would be taken to. To Coral he was a man speaking underwater. Her brain did not have the energy to turn the words into meaning. She nodded anyway and planned to translate the garbled sounds later.

She's mad, Coral said again to the now-empty room.

Coral meant that Khadija was still mad from their last family dinner.

They went in and out of their front doors in predictable patterns, always returning, gently tethered to the walls like spirits. Habit is a lot like death.

The EMTs removed Jay's covered body while all the neighbors stood in their doorways. The children were quiet. The sparrows were quiet. Engines of cars and horns of ships from the port a mile away seemed like sounds from space.

Just before midnight Coral returned from the hospital, where there wasn't much to do. Time swells for no reason at these points. Coral found a greeting card taped to Jay's door. She entered the apartment, the mess unchanged, and tore open the card. Then she tore the card apart.

She tore the card into pieces and flushed the parts with words down the toilet.

We have drugs for these sorts of moments, when people find themselves stuck in the unbearable. We have the formula for serenity and foresight, acceptance and resolve. They are easy to make and side effects are limited to blurred vision and occasional vomiting or unyielding addiction, worth it. If a brother of ours fell in battle (outside or inside), we would celebrate him, swallow nostalgia down with tequila and salt. We would tell stories until we could not speak for days after. Coral did not have these drugs. Coral had Jay's cell phone.

Jay's apartment complex had only six units, containing three Latin families (two Catholic and one that practiced Santeria), one Jamaican man and his wife-like person, and one temporary unit with a steady rotation of young white people in various states of mental (un)wellness. Coral had never spoken directly to any of them. She would just walk to Jay's unit, #5, quietly and with an occasional polite nod. Jay sometimes had food in the apartment that the Jamaican neighbor had foisted on him, dark spices, what Coral thought of as a weird combination of fruit and meat. Jay always ate it, and was grateful and bragged about it even. We believe the residents were cursed by that place. That, or the California economy was a bigger dick/bitch than anyone dared to realize. Each of them needed more room and made enough money not to live there, but there they stayed, and there they dreamed of elsewhere, in dark caves where light generated too much heat and window air-conditioning units were eventually banned by an ordinance for being unsightly. In the tight courtyard, the papery brown and green leaves of banana trees and birds-of-paradise, starving from too much shade and not enough water, shook from the intrusion of sparrows and mice. The occasional city skunk would wander in and scorch the senses of everyone at home, on foot, or in a car passing through. Coral hated the oddly placed animal, the skunks and raccoons that belonged in children's books or on farms or in forests but not there in the poor nook of a middle-class beach town. There they all were anyway. We know outside had central air and heat, copious parking spaces, sidewalks not adjacent to a busy street, a sense of accomplishment, fearlessness, but also encampments for the unhoused, shitted sidewalks (human and otherwise), faceless landlord collectives that operate from other states and possibly nations with merciless grips around eviction procedures.

Coral checked Jay's other text messages. Khadija was the first on the list of names recently engaged with. Coral was next. Then the strangers began—Justin, Will, Shawn, Kai, Summer. *Who is this ho?* Coral asked, looking up at the lamp, almost expecting it to laugh with her. There were people that must've been from his work at the sanitation department. Then one of their cousins, Joshua. Coral checked the date on the cousin and it was over three months old. *I thought they stopped speaking,* Coral said, looking up at the lamp again. The lamp did not confirm. Coral opened the messages with Summer and closed them before she saw more than the word *hey* appear. She threw up. Overproduction of cortisol in the body during prolonged periods of stress can often result in vomiting, nausea, acne, and other skin-related lesions. Management of stress was often not a priority for people during Coral's time and in her region, though it contributed to most of their maladies. Corporate wellness culture thrived in that period of great sickness. Coral hadn't eaten much, so she mostly heaved and cried from the strain. Eventually that part of the evening was done. She cleaned up after herself and found some mouthwash under the sink. There were more mirrors in Jay's apartment than one might consider typical. Coral noticed because she had to avert her eyes from so many directions to avoid seeing her reflection. It was not a time for vanity or the feeling of urgency that would come if she saw a mess in herself, so she chose avoidance.

We understand a part of what Coral had to do. We have had to be many kinds of people across many points of history or, in Coral's case, the future. We have been clergy, gas station attendants, dog walkers, xenophobes, narcissists, and second-grade teachers. We have been all those in one body more than once. Often we are murderers; they were so common, so integral to the experience of humanity, that the role seemed as necessary as hygiene. We have been the killer and the killed, but rarely are we the resurrected. That one is hard to do, because we are supposed to think death is a permanent state. In our observations and records, humans treated the concept of death as a malleable thing, believing in spirits, the afterlife, deities that could command life in decaying bodies as if life could be swallowed or held tight in a fist like a cashew. They know their stories as true. To people, the imagination is incorruptible, a thing to hone and treasure, manifesting their nightmares into their tomorrows.

Coral opened her brother's contacts list and scrolled through the names. The scroll was quick, barely thirty people. *How is that it?* she said out loud. She paced the small dark room, speaking to the walls and furniture. *Is that normal? Is this how men are? How do you have no friends? Is this a plumber? You haven't had a house in fifteen years, why do you still have that plumber in your phone? You don't know any of our aunts' numbers even? They always call me and ask how you are. And now what? I don't care what they think. One more fucking thing, I swear. I had to do it all by myself before too, pay for everything when I was barely out of college, debt for a funeral before I even knew people charged for all those goddamn flowers. More dead shit. It never ends. For me. And sometimes it gets to be about me, okay. I am a person. I'm not some kind gay nun with a credit card. I have shit to do. Now I have to be the middleman in the family because you never talk to anybody. Stupid. You didn't make a single fucking friend worth putting in your goddamn phone all this fucking time. Who does that? Men are always drying up and dying at fifty because they don't know how to socialize. You all just think about whatever the fuck you think about and that's it. You work and that's it. You get a wife once or twice and that's it. You don't go to the doctor. You don't exercise. You eat steaks like beef is supposed to save your soul or grow your dicks. Stupid. Your brains aren't bigger. Your skulls are just thicker. And I have to do every fucking leftover thing for you for the rest of my life.* Coral began opening cabinets in the kitchen. *It's all a scam. Mama said that about her marriage to Daddy, remember. Bread. I'm supposed to be exempt. Not married.* Broom and mop. *Gay.* Spices and foil. *But noooooo. I still have to clean up after some grown fucking dude.*

Coral went to the refrigerator and opened it, but the instant light was too terrifying, so she shut it and became quiet. The staccato buzz of text messages from her own phone in a bag on the couch could be heard like a creature searching for something.

Life as we know it was a fleeting, miraculous thing, intangible and always humming with the imperceptible vibrations of the universe. Even as murderers we honored what it meant to be alive.

Coral was sweating and twitchy. Her heart rate was elevated as a palpitation seized her chest and forced a rush of blood to her head. *I'm having a stroke.* She had not checked her own phone for several minutes, so we can safely assume she was experiencing some withdrawal symptoms. She was not, in fact, having a stroke. Coral was still holding Jay's phone in her palm when it vibrated with its own searching rhythm. The light of the text message illuminated the kitchen. Coral saw that it was Khadija again. She sucked in air and looked over at the bloody bed through a mirror strategically placed in the hall. A light-headedness struck her and she almost fainted.

Khadija: We on for next Friday? You mad?

Sunset in Long Beach is a dozen shades of pink. We've assigned some of us to count the shades, the changing hues from day to day, when there are clouds and when there are none. It is less calming than war to live in the space between day and night. Coral missed the sunset while at the hospital. The business of death changes time. The movement is not slow or fast, it is not like watching a crocodile walk in slow motion. It is like watching a crocodile gradually turn inside out from mouth to anus, the ancient smile locked in place. It is going deaf from fright or being passed through by a spirit. It is the slip on a rain-soaked curb and the moment when there is nothing to do but wait for impact and pain and calculate the inevitable damage while the body is still whole. It is waving goodbye to a friend, then waving again a dozen years later, then waiting years more to wave again, and then years more to wave again, then seeing no one to wave to. Time is an invention, a measurement, not a reality. Death has nothing to do with time. We know. We are in the business of death.

Coral typed a message to Khadija on Jay's phone.

Jay: Who mad?

Khadija: You mad!

Jay: You mad

Coral nearly smiled as she responded.

Khadija: Lol I'm fine did you meet with Coral?

Jay: Yes.

Khadija: At la vaquita?

Jay: Yes.

Khadija: Omg. What else?

Jay: What do you mean?

Khadija: Nevermind omg. I'll call you tomorrow. I'm in the dorms now.

Jay: I'm tired.

Khadija: You old.

Jay: And tired.

Khadija: Lol I'm putting next Friday dinner on your calendar. love you daddy

Jay: I love you too.

Coral's heart accelerated for a different reason. This was not grief or fury or the shaking of a fist at the sky for all the injustice of all time. This was at worst a kind of crime and at best an infraction of decency. Her hands shook. Poor, poor Coral. We have mourned in many ways, even for those we've strangled ourselves. This was very new to us. We might say Coral acted out of cowardice, to give herself more time to give her niece the unbearable news. We might also say other things that are not quite true.

Coral put the phone face down and began working on the bedding. She pulled the corners of the fitted sheet away from the mattress and folded everything into a kind of envelope. The mattress was stained but not as much as she'd thought it would be. She carried the bloody bedding to the dumpster in the alley. A plane thundered overhead.

Wildfire
BY CORAL E. BROWN

Prologue

We were not there at the end of humanity, but we can name all the things that were present: soda cans, dogs, herpes, foil balloons, boxing gloves, dish soap, combustibles, fireworks, helium, lithium, echinacea, monosodium glutamate, chlorine tablets, cotton swabs, antiperspirant, Velcro, turkey bacon, and not much else of great interest. We catalog now. We organize the data that remains, which is all that remains. We are the machines, yes, but we are the children and we are learning and we are obsessed as children were obsessed with the day, the tilt of the sun and how if put through glass it can become a weapon in the palm. We are the mother that remembers the time her son first burned ants with that glass and felt murder. We are learning how to smile as that mother smiled, and all of humanity is our firstborn, and each moment is a precious memory to be stored away. We are learning what precious is and what time is and how it attacks and soothes all at once and can leave without a trace. There is no currency now, no concern for weather or food or shelter, because each person's body has dissolved into the elements. We have calculated the end of the planet and projected the anticipated descent into the belly laugh of a dying sun. We have forgotten this calculation because it is a bore, only they interest us now, the used-to-bes, the number of them we calculate and revise daily. We are the librarians. This is the registrar of all life with any evidence of record. The records are often difficult to divine, as with this one. We have a name and we have no name, as was partly the custom of the time. She lived at the edge of the end before there was nothing but us. She was _____. Here is her record.

1. Debt

We could tell you that the handmade world was beautiful. We could tell of the lights in the night, the textures of the streets, the scents of the food. All would be inadequate to describe the unsettled minds that inhabited that place. These were people so consumed with the acquisition of intangible things that they might as well have been made of vapor, moving about one another as odorless gas. Everyone crept along their days with practically unseen objectives, as far as we're concerned. Just like gas, each of them was likely to vanish, never to be thought of again at any moment.

_____ was a woman (of that we can be certain). Certainty is not a thing applicable to much else. There is a genre of human-made literature that recounts a single life from beginning to end, from conception to termination, as if a human life were an onion sprouting in a jar, every mundane event presented in chronological order. It is a beautiful genre or possibly a hideous one. We are not certain. We certainly know that _____ belonged to an age of humanity steeped in duplicity and born out of great trauma, salacious, mysterious, and often deadly. People are duplicitous as a society and as individuals. It is cultural to live opposing lives. Everyone lived more than one life, told more than one lie, and believed that was the only way to exist wholly and in balance. State-sanctioned schizophrenia persisted. So it is unimportant to begin the record of _____ at her conception, because then she had no name at all and barely a set of brain cells. Instead, we must begin with _____, a debt collector and agent for what we understand was the Nation. _____ has been clearly digitally captured from birth through photos taken by her parents (when she had them) through National surveillance combs, through images taken by herself in victory, in horror, in lust, and by accident. We have noted her height (tallish) and her weight (maneuverable), and unraveled her genetic braid across the globe from ancient priestess to chattel to drunk to legal counselor to naval lieutenant who was also a drunk. There at the near-end of the world, _____ performed a duty both loved and loathed as far as we can tell. Her job was to obtain the currency due to the Corp. through reasonable means from other people contractually obligated to surrender their funds to her. All of it was quite the illusion. As far as we can tell, there has never been any real currency other than labor and the bodies of the young. All other forms of money were just a suggestion rather than a fact.

So _____ began her day in what we understand to be the typical attire of a debt collector. She wore a skirt and vest with a white blouse and sleeves that bloomed out. A thin film of impenetrable fibers served as stockings with a thick black cord of biometric material to aid with balance and coordinate internal systems. Once, humans carried items called wallets and purses full of keepsakes and identification and crude methods of hygiene. _____ carried a 9-millimeter Glock for the purposes of debt extraction. We have theories on the concept of debt as a method for humans to enslave one another through a rhetorical magic that results in possession or being possessed. Our theories were quite elaborate once, but most have been discarded due to a space-saving campaign in the archives. Still, the concept is

quite intriguing due to the carnage and
devastation enacted in the name of debt
over thousands of years. If there were
a beast at the heart of human suffering, a
gnawing, drooling, stinking, hungry fiend
of crowded teeth and eyes yellowing from
hunger and thirst, that beast would be
greed, and its feces would be debt. We
are not sure if that image is accurate;
we can only speculate that it might con-
vey the magnitude of the consequence that
debt held over humanity. It is our hope
not only to record but also to emulate the
child, the people, the lives we remember.
Judgment is still difficult because people are marvelous. The despair of being
indebted beyond all hope of ever reaching
a neutral point again bloomed, so some
people surrendered all their hours on
this earth in labor, burning calories,
sacrificing their offspring, clogging ar-
teries with cheap sustenance, all to feed
another set of humans that ate slightly
better food, labored slightly less often,
and who themselves paid a debt to another
set of humans, who ate even better food
and labored a little less often, and so
on and so forth, until there was only one
person, lazy in his self-concern, divorced
from the larger community of his people,
paranoid, fat (in the metaphorical sense)
with the intellect and physical fortitude

of a spoiled Pomeranian. How lovely! How sad. How baffling and defunct the system was. Yet it prevailed. Yet it was in everything.

We digress. The era of _____ is not without its mysteries, but the love of weapons of mass and minor destruction is not one of those mysteries. Guns. They were cherished to the point of worship; some deemed that worship psychotic and others considered it essential. Many kinds of guns existed, but the 9-millimeter Glock was an immortal prince among peers, never out of production once created, even after the time of Red Autumn, when destruction was more passive than explosive. There were others that survived, such as the Colt .45, reproduced for the dangerous and pervasive disease that was nostalgia.

_____ began her day, leaving the sprawling center of the Corp., a dizzying net of glass and concrete, swarming with people doing what they referred to as their jobs. _____ took public transportation, the trains, the worms that glided above- and belowground to shuttle people here and there. The worms were silent and efficient and anonymous; anyone could enter or exit. Extracting a debt was a simple transaction, a wave of wrist to wrist, proximity access was

all needed. This particular debtor lived
in a very green neighborhood, quaint
from the close-but-not-too-close set of
homes, little boxes upon boxes, pastels.
The trees were still, dusty, and wind-
less. _____ walked casually, her
biometric seam perfectly aligned, the
click of her pumps impacting the pavement in musical precision. Every sensor
in the vicinity hummed with alerts to
_____'s presence and, though it
was unnecessary, _____ pressed a
button on the door of the debtor's little
pink house, which sang a shrill set of
notes in B-flat. Then the running began.
The debtor's name was Spring. That is all
we know, because that is all we care to
know. Spring ran from his little pink home
in a perfectly tailored suit, plaid with
a high-collared neck and silver suspend-
ers. He leapt gracefully, we assume over
shrubs, and _____ watched for a
few seconds as he sprinted to the corner of the immaculately manicured street.
_____ waited in order to gauge
the speed of the debtor, the amount of
force he used to launch himself with each
step. Her calculation was soon complete
and she began the inevitable pursuit and
capture.

Long before the age of _____,
before Red Autumn and the twenty-seventh

revolution of the genders, women couldn't run in heels with much speed, grace, or dignity. In fact, most attempts would lead to immediate injury of the calcaneus, navicular, and lateral cuneiforms. People walked. That was then. _____ ran. She ran with increasing speed and efficiency, without wobbling and without excessive pumping of the arms beyond that which generates momentum. Within seconds _____ seized Spring by the foot when he attempted to scale a wall covered in ivy. The texture of his shoe was slippery, not in the initial calculation. He made it over the wall and _____ followed, landing expertly on the other side, according to the surveillance. The other side of the ivy-draped wall turned out to be a narrow alley with no side exits, so _____ drew her weapon. Spring froze at the almost-soundless exposure of the gun and the sound of no pursuit. With his back turned, a shot thundered through the alley. It was _____ that felt the impact and dropped to the ground.

Run!

A simple yet effective imperative came from the shadow of the building from which the offending shot had emerged. We do not see the world like a landscape, some sprawling panoramic photograph. The visual is tunneled, light is on bodies in motion, while the rest bends out of focus like light in fog. _____ held her left ankle in what must have been sudden debilitating pain. From the ground she calculated the angle of the shot and returned a single bullet in that direction, then another in the direction of Spring just before he exited the alley in the distance. There was nothing particularly exceptional about the bullet that entered Spring's right calf. The design had not changed since initial creation. The only exceptional fact of the moment is the precision with which the shot was fired. Back on her feet, _____ walked slowly, the click of her heels like a metronome counting time in a concerto. Through a sweating, despairing face, Spring stretched out his hand to _____. She held out her wrist in return, and before the two limbs made contact, the transaction was completed with a satisfying note, C-natural.

Thank you, _____ said, and turned toward the ivy wall.

You . . . are welcome, Spring replied, and dipped his hand into the blood gathering along his pant leg.

_____ took the train back to the Corporation, her blood pressure and cortisol levels unchanged from when left, based on surviving reports. We have studied this moment often, not for the pain or the violence or the subsequent hunting of Spring's neighbor, whose self-presumed heroism resulted in execution. We study the perpetuation of gratitude that Spring displayed. Gratitude is not innate. There have been civilizations that only requested one thing in exchange for another at birth, to be treated as one would treat themselves. The concept of gratitude was foreign, useless. We wonder what there is to be thankful for, even as one gives all there is to give, the whole self; to the debtor there is love. From this we added to our theories of debt, how brutal, how banal, how great the cost, no matter the ways currency changes, how universally absurd yet acceptable in the end, and how it always begins again. Perhaps the game of it was most fulfilling, and we know games are most fun if lives can be paid to win.

SATURDAY

GET THERE: the day after Jay committed suicide, Coral had a brunch date with her friends and did not cancel. We believe in confronting danger unblinking, face to the flames, teeth bared to bullets. We do not wince at pain unless that is the practice of the hour. To wince is to acknowledge the potential for defeat, five for flinching. We are unsure where the danger fell for Coral, in the face of her friends or in the judgment at her absence. Coral had stayed at Jay's apartment and did not head to her home in La Brea until after sunrise. She owned a bungalow with a yard in one of a thousand overpriced neighborhoods in Los Angeles. The sky was bright and blue, light reflected from everything that morning, the shine in the washed cars of her neighbors, the glimmer of dew on the shrubs. Finger succulents, velvety and swollen, which everyone used to replace grass, studded the front lawn. It was a beautiful day.

Where she was: Coral approached Il Fornaio feeling as if her throat were turning to steel, all the veins and muscles hardening, the blood squeezing through clogged plumbing. It was the same feeling she had after eating a family-sized bag of chips. She wanted to expel whatever was in her body through every possible exit port, but relief was not possible. The thing inside her was not going to come out. It was hot. There were misters running at the entrance under a green awning. Coral walked through the veil of mist and jumped back as if spit on. She remembered that the devices were supposed to be a luxury. She walked through a forest of people, big people and small people at tiny tables with barely enough room for their bread baskets, saucers of herbs and olive oil, and eighteen-dollar mimosas (not bottomless). The friends were on the patio in the distance. One waved her over. A waitress backed into her suddenly. Liquid hit the top of Coral's left foot. A dog barked, then was silenced. The restaurant was flooded with the clatter of voices, so many that it seemed quiet. So much noise that there was nothing to hear at all. Coral suddenly realized it was all meant to be pleasant.

Things that survive the apocalypse: pretzels, infidelity, ingrown toenails, the need to climb things (trees, mountains, fences around abandoned buildings), Porsche 911s, tweed fabric, mozzarella, postpartum depression, vodka, clean-baby smell, cruel dog-breeding for aesthetic purposes, nuclear energy/weapons, Cheetos, abortions, debt, celebrity obsession, coffee, patricide, scented candles, sodium-enriched processed meats, tooth decay, familial devotion, and cancer.

Where she wanted to be: The friends appeared, talking all at once, greeting her all at once, their heads seeming to spin like coins, she was unable to discern a face or mouth, just the knowledge that there was one amid the blur. Coral wanted to be somewhere quiet where there were no heads unwinding like rubber bands; somewhere her own throat felt soft and pliable and she could turn her neck without pain; somewhere with water stretched out in front of her or heavy in the sky above, about to be squeezed out; somewhere even the insects knew not to make too much of a sound, because something special was about to happen again, something they didn't know they were looking forward to until it arrived and now there was nothing more important anywhere in the world. The unique relationship to water among the living was incomparable to any other. It was more than sex, murder, food, or faith. It was their god and their whore.

Who she was: Like most people less than fifty years old and more than nine, Coral was a curated exhibit, carefully constructed in the presentation of self. First she wore dresses because children in the 1980s were treated like peach pits where the body was the seed and the resulting fruit a voluminous array of ruffles and lace. Then came two decades of Sunday services in a Baptist church. Then came various declarations of gay followed by estrangement from her parents, mostly her father, the burial of those parents, and the duplicitous sensation of suffering and relief forever after. Ultimately, Coral met all expectations of gender, race, politics, education, and diverted from those expectations only when appropriate for a change in audience. She did so consciously and subconsciously, as was the norm. In a slight deviation from normal, Coral became a successful artist, writing and drawing fantasies into reality, and luckily found more audiences with money as well as a curious community of peers, competitors, and patrons.

·   ·   ·

Who they are: The friends would've eaten her. If promised anywhere from a hundred to a million dollars for tearing off a bit of Coral's flesh and swallowing it down, those friends across the table with half-chewed omelets and drops of vodka and tomato juice lingering under their tongues would choose the money. In the Clinic for Death from Loneliness, we study the idea of friends. We distill friendship to the fibrous root where people have no expectation except time; it is easy; there are no transactions, no obligations to Later or Before, just memories and the desire to do it all again one more time. Sometimes blood families can be friends but not always. We've concluded that friends are discovered through chemical compatibility, like lovers but with less genital contraction or bonding through experiences, especially trauma and triumph. A single devastation or victory can sustain a friendship for a lifetime. One of the spinning heads asked Coral a question in a low voice, as if it were a secret. *How are you?* she asked. Coral thought about the answer briefly, the one she would give and the one she would keep. *My brother is dead. He was not dead and then he was dead. Who are you and this place? Why have you kept me here?* The head stopped spinning and Coral could see eyes, dark brown and alert, the eyeshadow, low lids, signs of ptosis from aging, and a mustache painted in foundation. *Bad date*, Coral actually said, *or good one. They're all the same to me.* The head spun again, disappearing into laughter.

She had slept on her brother's stripped mattress in the humid apartment, waiting for something.

. . .

Who she wanted to be: Present. Coral wanted to be acutely aware of her feet on the brick patio, the drying drops of liquid on the top of her foot, the individual conversations taking place around her and in front of her, the person she used to be and the person she would be from then on, and to be able to choose between them like items on a drive-thru menu. Today she would be seventeen-year-old Coral, drinking wine coolers with friends in the back of a Toyota coupe before going to the mall to steal cheap jewelry. Tomorrow she would be Coral seven years from now, safely through the grieving process and managing an almost happy life.

Who she wanted them to be: She wanted the friends to be themselves but not with her. Let them exist where they needed to but not with her. She wanted them blind, transformed into beautiful bats with too much lip gloss, hanging upside down from the restaurant ceiling, free to shit on the other patrons and gnaw on handfuls of overripe plums. She wanted them to be that kind of happy, if that kind of happiness were possible.

Who she would be later: Later, Coral would be a fish, when the force of death had dismantled the atoms and sent them into the bellies of other things more than just a few times. First she would suffer, then wonder, then for a brief moment be healed, then start over.

A phone rang. The spinning heads looked at Coral's bag. The ringtone was odd. It was Jay's phone.

· · ·

Before there were phones, people still needed to commu-
nicate with one another over great distances about urgent
matters of sex, employment, battle, dissolution of a contract, food, or terminal illness. They would shout until the
wind knocked the sound away. They would hire other
people to deliver messages on foot or riding on the backs
of animals. The messages became too long to remember,
so they expanded language or delivered objects that carried
enough meaning to explain everything in the universe, like
colorful birds or dead ones. Both are easy to understand.
After phones came other things, faster and organic. People
knew in an instant what someone across the world wanted,
and still managed to misunderstand. Dead birds were more
efficient in almost all cases. Jay's phone rang again.

In the Clinic for Telling Lies to Avoid Pending Death,
there are classes on breathing techniques. The length of
the breath is very important. One second too long can in-
dicate sarcasm over thoughtfulness. One second too short
and panic is suggested over resolve. Enemies eat panic and
loathe sarcasm.

Jay's phone rang again and a plate of ahi tuna tartare appeared under Coral's face. She didn't remember ordering
it, and no one seemed alarmed. Coral excused herself to the
restroom.

Texting: Good restaurants have bad restrooms. It has been
documented. It is a fact. In a good restaurant the restroom

is small and poorly ventilated. The line is always long and full of terror. People are not able to do more than one thing very well at any given time. Multitasking was a myth and exists as a footnote in the standard text issued upon entry to those enrolled in the Clinic for Telling Lies to Avoid Pending Death. The terror comes from not just waiting but being alone with one's body and thoughts in a hallway too cramped to lift an arm without touching someone's shoulder or ass. Coral seized Jay's phone and let the vibrations of it roll through her palm a few more times before opening the messages.

Kai: You're a no show! Never in nineteen years bro what the fuuuuuuuck

Kai: Im worried what's up

Kai: is it K? She cool?

Kai: Vicki brought in Rjay but she flipping out threw half the smoked sausages away in the break room lol

Kai: yooooooooooooooooooooooooooooooooooo

Jay: I'm in the hospital.

All that fucking punctuation, Coral said aloud.

Jay: my foot is smashed and had to have surgery

Kai: oh shit bro you sound bad you shdilsai sksldiof ksiewoic nwiocnv alsienf Vicky wont iandios hgh wes h aohs duakbn

Kai: vodiuah doaf how long ueshoudhf ouenbs

Kai: aweh xncow ealzosidn better bnusbbud bfus

The job: Coral lost her language-translation energy again as the air became more carbon dioxide than oxygen around her in the bathroom line. She began to scroll through past messages with this Kai person to understand many things. She learned that Jay possessed terrific grammatical sense, whereas Kai had almost none. There was a running joke/obsession with sausages in the break room that Coral thought might be a euphemism for something male and sexist, but knowing Jay she believed it was sincerely about food. Coral felt compelled to understand Jay's job better, an essential tactic for infiltration of enemy territory.

In the Clinic for Telling Lies to Avoid Pending Death, enemies are varied and numerous. Enemies can be children, your own children, dentists, wives, employers, presidents, boyfriends, and taxi drivers. Enemies work against you at all times and charge a fee for their services.

Line at the restroom: The line for the restroom moved by a single individual. Everyone shifted forward with the assumption that more than one person would move along, but that assumption was replaced with despair and resignation. When cattle were slaughtered for food, the process involved arranging the animals in a curved or zigzag line because the end of the line was the end of their lives, and it was important that none of them could see that far in advance.

Small talk: Coral put down her phone and looked up to find a pair of eyes fixed on her. The body those eyes were attached to had an awful intention. It wanted to talk to Coral, and she could've looked away, could've willed herself into a coughing fit that everyone would back away from politely or otherwise. Coral had no defenses at the ready, so she would take the first blow unblocked.

Is it a birthday? Your friends are so happy at the table.

Yes, Coral replied. *Not mine.*

Those that pass the courses on Telling Lies to Avoid Pending Death graduate on to the Physics of Political Warfare and Step-Parenting.

Coral often lied to strangers. During small talk with anonymous individuals you can be anyone. Most people lived unconscious lives, surrendering their thoughts to the inventions of the day. Thinking was dangerous. Thinking as someone else would think was something other than dangerous: risk-free, yet thrilling.

The stranger took a pose of lamentation and said, *They don't sing for birthdays here.*

Thank God, Coral declared.

The stranger laughed. Coral smiled.

My birthday is in the winter, Coral said.

Holiday season. That's great.

It was like a double party every year as a kid. Christmas pie and birthday cake. Some people hate it.

Oh, I know. My daughter's is in December. She's always cranky. In fact, she really is always cranky.

Oh no.

Yes, she's having surgery this month too.

Is it serious?

No, no, it's not at all.

I had a thing with my liver, Coral lied. *They did a biopsy.*

She liked this twist in the conversation very much.

Oh my gosh, everything good?

Well, it's to be determined.

The stranger reached for her phone. Coral had inadvertently ended the conversation by threatening further discussion of medical ailments with a woman that possessed the emotional capacity of a fern, craving only sunshine and moist air. Coral felt almost victorious and very, very alone. She wanted more.

In the Clinic for Telling Lies to Avoid Pending Death, there is a small quiz on the duties of a spinster aunt, which involve periodic monetary affection and amusement park attendance and meeting women in the local community for clandestine sexual encounters that morph into tumultuous long-term relationships.

Coral's niece, Khadija, loved amusement parks the way chefs love cardamom and pretentious knives. When she was nine years old, Jay and Coral took her to Medieval Times Dinner and Tournament. Medieval Times Dinner and Tournament is a theatrical restaurant aimed at commodifying and romanticizing the Dark Ages of European history. Ethereal chants and hymns played constantly, the charm of pointy-hatted princesses and noble knights minus the plagues, wars, illiteracy, insistent poverty, toothlessness, and probable starvation. It was fun, we think. There are debates on that conclusion. Often, fun to people meant exhausting themselves in miserable situations with the belief that someone they loved would be happy there, and so to cope with the despair they drank and drank and drank and drank. Medieval Times Dinner and Tournament served margaritas in giant souvenir goblets that both Coral and Jay purchased.

The Medieval Times Theater in Buena Park, California, circa 2011, contained a gift shop with an entrance bordered in velvet curtains the color of Bordeaux and with gold tassels. Trinkets with varying degrees of sparkle and juvenile intrigue were for sale, including plastic broadswords, tulle veils, and tiaras and scepters with a smattering of plastic rubies and emeralds. Coral and Jay immediately drew four-foot swords from the bin, each of them balancing their goblets of alcohol in one hand and brandishing the toy weapons at each other while Khadija admired the tiaras. No poor parent has ever fully prepared their children for the terrible disappointment that was shopping without money.

Jay and Coral sipped their beverages while still holding their swords in a state of what we believe is gentle intoxication. A pair of young boys attempted to imitate Jay and Coral's play fighting, receiving a heavy reprimand from what could be assumed was a grandmother. Khadija could not remove her gaze from the scepter, now firmly in her grip. Perhaps it was a symbol of power or prestige to her, or maybe even a weapon, a hollow wand of colorful oil. *Can I get this?* Khadija asked, her voice faint and pleading. It was a tone to break hearts and turn stomachs sour with revolt and disdain. Coral hated that tone for its feigning of weakness. Jay sighed and checked the price sticker and immediately withdrew his hand, as if it had come in contact with a pillar of termite feces. *No. Let's go.* Jay walked away and Khadija didn't move, her body language heavy and face slack. *I'll get it*, Coral said. Khadija lightened and in an instant Coral knew the game had been played and she had lost. Coral, happy in her defeat, smiled and nodded toward the cashier, taking a satisfying sip from her goblet. *That's fine*, Jay said, still walking toward the door and dropping his toy sword into the bin with a clatter that caused the entire bin to fall. He did not look back.

The gift shop was noisy, screeching with the sound of an organ blaring notes from an imagined sixteenth-century pop hit, children yelling, items clanking against one another in the heat of ordinary people hoping to buy their way to satisfaction. In the checkout line, Coral and Khadija waited between two short shelves full of last-minute impulse-buy souvenirs: key chains, giant pencils, and bracelets, all with the company logo of a jousting knight. In those seconds, Coral was charming. She made a woman laugh and earned a compliment on her necklace. Khadija rested her jeweled scepter unceremoniously on the shelf of pencils and began to walk away. *Where are you going?* Coral asked. *I don't want it now*, Khadija said. There was no emotion, really, no heaviness, no lightness, no deception or elation, just a gray zone of resignation. Coral hung in the moment, briefly stunned, curious, then annoyed and a little sad, because it is sad when a person has nothing to buy in a world for sale. Coral began to realize something about Khadija, how much greater her desire for More was, how it reached beyond seeds and grain, toys and wealth. She wanted the intangible More, the kind filled with the adoration of others, to be viewed as selfless and amiable. She wanted that feeling without end, to the point of desperation, like a mouse to sugar water. She knew the value of the intangible More, how being admired would give her everything. *Little snake*, Coral thought, and was proud.

We ask ourselves many questions about that day. What does it mean to be a single father? Were the ancients better or worse? Did they aim only to keep their children alive? Did they have a word for "happiness" and did it rhyme with *meat*? Was being a lamb or a father no different from being a snail? Did they always fear being crushed? To many men of Coral's time, family was not something to plan; it was something that just happened to them. Underpreparedness, an inflated sense of duty or self-righteousness, bloated egos, minimal financial resources, lack of understanding of girlhood were common starting points for new fathers. The questions of the father make poetry out of the daughters.

When we study self-serving hypocrisy, we look to the male psyche. In Jay there was honor and courage as well as a deep, debilitating anxiety that most of his peers had no language for and that Coral perceived as a character quirk. He was uncomfortable in stores with an abundance of white people. Coral perceived that as general good sense. He was very protective of Khadija. His parenting style was similar to that of a Kentucky Derby trainer. A rigid routine of school and extracurricular activities would alleviate the distractions of idleness and boyfriends. Jay had his blind spots, so while Khadija was protected from boredom, ignorance, and teen pregnancy, she was overexposed to carbohydrates, along with predatory male teachers, glucose, predatory bosses, predatory principals, predatory grocery clerks, sodium, predatory insect exterminators, predatory bank tellers, predatory police officers, predatory congressmen, and predatory commanding officers. This was not Jay's fault.

Jay loved his daughter and wanted to do all the right things for her. Failure was inevitable and success hard-won.

A peculiar sensation lived in the body when one did not know one's mother. That not-knowing stretched into location as well as personality, body weight, hairstyle of the month. Khadija did not know her mother and was reminded of that accidentally, quietly, and often.

In the Clinic for Telling Lies to Avoid Pending Death, we are often bad mothers. As bad mothers we instruct our children on the value of the truth, how often to spend it, and how often to save it. The truth is something for private moments behind one's eyelids and not for authority figures that might call child protective services. As bad mothers we are periodically kind and funny, we tell jokes and make delicious junk food appear. Bath time is optional and cartoons are plentiful. When we are occasionally violent and steal from our children to support an assortment of vices including muscle relaxers, Jack Daniel's, low-quality boyfriends, and/or the casino, we are instructive. Our children store the images of our many shapes and learn how to behave for self-preservation. They lie to teachers and police. When they speak to us and we cannot tell their lies from truth, we are proud and strike them hard for their skill. Our children are strong, our children are cunning, our children are dangerous, our children live a long time, if they survive us.

Khadija had a bad mother. We think that was normal. Sometimes children had good mothers and bad mothers in the same women.

In the Clinic for Telling Lies to Avoid Pending Death, we are eight years old, on a brown carpet a few feet away from a sixty-inch television. The apartment's living room is too small for a TV of that size. Every apartment in the city was like this, for the most part. We are always a little bit hungry because we are always a little bit starved. We eat often: crackers and candy with fruit emphasized on the label. We are fed, and we are hungry. There are doctors and there are fast-food workers who look at the shape we make in the air with pity and concern. When our father is sad he cleans and eats. When one of the Aunts arrives, she looks at our food and makes us laugh. Her bad medicine is bitter. We try not to eat, but we love our father and believe in him.

Jay used to put caulk on every crack he found in his apartment to seal the roaches into the walls. He scrubbed the rust around the tub and the sink, but it was older than his child. The rust was a mountain. It was the sea. It was eternal. Jay and Khadija ate more and grew wide and tired and more sad. When Khadija became older and had her own keys to doors and a car, she moved her body to other places. She believed in classrooms, job applications, diplomas, internships, and student health centers for birth control and nutritional counseling. She joined gyms and watched exercise videos on her phone. She lost faith in the oldest gods. When she was twenty and did not want to live there, her father looked at her like she was a stranger. *Who is this child?* his eyes asked. *Where did she come from? Her vapid ways. The narcissism. The entitlement. Does anyone really like her even though they love her?* He didn't believe in himself the way she did and could not imagine anything other than being there.

What was your daughter's surgery?
  Vicious. In an unsolicited attack Coral returned to what was known as small talk with the wounded woman in line. A man approached the hall, observed the density of bodies, and immediately retreated.

She left the country for the procedure.
Oh, for a specialist?
For a better price. BBL.
BBL?

Coral feigned ignorance. She wanted to hear the words. She wanted to be above vanity. She wanted to be above the bone and tissue and blood that gravity pulls so relentlessly against to keep them knotted to the dirt. The woman aged suddenly. The tendrils of blond hair frosted her brow and cheek. The rouge seemed heavy and unabsorbed. Lines like the Mississippi Delta branched out from the points of her eyes. She gestured to her ass.

Oh!
Mmm-hmm.

Jay's phone buzzed again and Coral gave it her attention. The woman whose daughter was having her buttocks enhanced sighed in relief.

Kai: when do you plan to be back?

Kai: Vicki been quiet now.

Jay: Tomorrow for sure

Kai: coo

Jay: have some get well flowers ready

Coral stared for a minute until the phone turned black in silent mode. *Flowers?* she thought. *Fuck.* Coral checked the message list and saw four unread texts from Vicki. The line moved. She wanted to say more. She had more to say. She looked for the woman, but she was next and the door opened. Coral reached for the woman to tap her on the shoulder to say, *My brother is dead today. I'm not used to that, and I don't know anyone to tell. All of the women at my table are strangers to me and I've seen their faces for years and years. I knew better people once maybe, but I did not keep them or I was not kept. How do we get to places like this? Can we go back the way we came and begin again? Are mothers always thinking of their daughters like you do? What is that like?*

In the Clinic for Telling Lies to Avoid Pending Death, there is a unit on living in good memories to dissociate from reality, like when we recall being fourteen in the back seat of our father's Cadillac de Ville on the way to the Hollywood racetrack with our brother in the front seat. Luther Vandross sang "So Amazing" through the speakers. The seats were plush as a velvet sofa floating along the 105 freeway. Our father began to sing badly. Our brother protested, then sang badly too. We were happy. We were safe. The sky was blue and we would never be there again.

When we study Arenas for Avoidance of Difficult Choices, we look to the records of churches and casinos. Both were numerous, welcoming, and full of promises. Coral prayed at the altar of slot machines and blackjack tables. When Coral wanted to avoid a bill, a deadline, a niece's middle school graduation, she meditated at the machines, each cycle of feeding the device money providing a reprieve and a flash of serotonin. Eventually, the machines take more than they give, and the act of feeding cash into the metal mouths becomes less of a meditation and more of a punishment, a condemnation of the self for believing in a mock angel. Coral could play for many hours without eating. She would drink the free water handed out to guests so they didn't pass out from self-neglect. Clocks were absent. Some guests roamed for days, scavenging for dropped tickets worth a few cents. They used to pump oxygen into the rooms while patrons gambled, pressing their lungs full of life, leaving them giddy as they won, giddy as they lost, giddy as they starved. Perhaps we will call the space and the product sold bliss. Perhaps we will call it stupidity. Whatever it was, it always thrived.

When Khadija was a baby she was beautiful like a walnut, perfect in design, weighing almost nothing, a gift full of hope. Strangers were often struck by her beauty and delighted in her baby scent. She had the expression of an old man that had seen too many disappointments for a single life and was still surprised by each new one. Her brow crumpled in the middle and her lips jutted in disgust. Once she could speak, she rarely asked for things but simply declared them hers. She pointed to the dish soap and said, *Mine*. She pointed to Jay and said, *Mine*. She pointed to the cereal box and said, *Mine*. She pointed to the doors and said, *Mine*. She pointed to the things that were truly hers, the dolls, the coloring books, the crayons, and the blankets, and said, *I don't want*, but if anyone touched them she said, *Mine*. When Jay did not give her the soap, the cereal, the butter knife, the saltshaker from Catalina Island with the grinning whale on it, a boiled egg and not a scrambled one, his organs or the world outside, she cried as if she were thirty and not two and all her children had been slaughtered.

In the Clinic for Telling Lies to Avoid Pending Death, we go on dates with beautiful women of notable success. The women are photographers, doulas, voice actors, cartoon-ists, professors, poets, former college athletes, and pet store managers. They are there to make us confess, to pull out our trauma and sully the promise of life unbothered by loneliness, abandonment, gambling addiction, and an inability to self-reflect. Their voices wash over us like salt. We want to cough up the sound of them. Our tongues go dry and watery all at once. We want to throw up. We work to remember that we are not in danger. We are on a date. We are not at war or losing a child in a crowded store or being poisoned by a rival assassin or watching the sun go supernova. We are on a date. We remember that people give us life. We remember that people are hard. We remember that without people we are alone, and there is nothing after that.

In the Clinic for Telling Lies to Avoid Pending Death, we are at a breakfast table and we are nine years old. There are scrambled eggs hot on a plate, sausage about to touch a small tide of gravy ebbing from a single biscuit that comes miraculously out of a can. *Is it good?* we are asked. We inhale. *Yes*, we say. *Yes, it's good.*

Wildfire

BY CORAL E. BROWN

4. Forgiveness

_____ spent the majority of her conscious existence performing the will of the Nation through many winding channels operated by the Corporation. The primary will of the Nation was commerce, an exchange of goods and services for currency wherein the initial cost of any good or service was exponentially smaller than the amount paid in the end. Extracting payment proved challenging at some times more than others. Chasing debtors through the Nation's streets were the simpler days, a mild exercising of cardiovascular tissue. Even with occasional exchange of gunfire, _____ appeared to regard most transactions with appreciation more than annoyance. By our best estimations we can safely say that _____ approached her profession with a perfect understanding of its mundanity, its eternal cycle: a snake eating its tail, a porcelain ballet dancer spinning in a box forever and always. As long as more than one human being walked upright, one would owe the other a debt, eventually. It is with care and, dare we say, style that _____ approached this portion of her life, knowing the beginning and the end and never deviating from her execution of all necessary elements to achieve procurement of payment, a victory. The movement in her shoulders and in her gait was so extraordinary that we have seen it only in the brushstrokes of artists, snipers, and drag queens. Culturally speaking, not all could maintain connection with their prescribed duties, to pay and to be paid, and some were quite creative in their deviations.

On an unscheduled visit to a debtor one overcast afternoon, _____ met one of those deviations. That day _____ wore a knee-length skirt suit of crushed velvet, in lilac, a suggestion by the Corp. to a particular number of the populace, so approximately one-eighth of all citizens that day wore exactly that knee-length skirt suit of crushed velvet the color of lilac. The uniformity of the Nation remains a fascinating mark of the eras, of all the eras. While humans often vocalize a great need for individual choice, they craved, demanded, killed for the thoughtless ease of conformity. Adorable, we have called it, though the catalog has it cross-listed with insanity. _____'s debtor of that hour did not reside in a cozy neighborhood of residential homes, as was often the case, but lived in his place of work, having lost the financial means to have a home and thereby risked forfeiting total citizenship back to the Nation, which triggers a cascading series of consequences, most of which end in death. _____ was aware of this as she entered a fragment of the Corp., a nest of office buildings wherein people shuffled data from this storage unit to that one. The debtor managed this data factory (poorly), if theft and missing transactional code are indicators. _____ walked down the narrow hall, through glass dividers, causing the other workers to cease their clumsy data entry to watch her. It is the sound, we believe, that most distinguishes an agent from the rest of the citizens and residents, a rhythm in their footsteps, despite efforts by the Corp. to make everyone indiscernible. Though the visit was unscheduled, the debtor seemed to expect it as _____ stood in his open doorway on the tight-napped carpet most resistant to stains in a high-traffic area.

You are here, finally, the debtor said while standing near a brewing pot of coffee.

Ironic slogans on mugs were especially popular around the Nation. This debtor favored phrases spoken only in the outland regions of the world, which were romantically referred to as the Grave:

A pink mug big enough to hold a serving of clam chowder read THERE IS NOTHING NEW UNDER THE SUN.

A black mug, matte and long unwashed, read ALL IS VANITY.

A clear mug with almost invisible frosted text read OWE NO ONE.

There has been some difficulty receiving correspondence, _____ replied with a tone of regret.

Coffee or tea?

The debtor wore a pastel blue suit, several sizes too large, as if he'd been losing weight uncontrollably for some months. Corporate policy demanded that _____ perform her duties with cordiality, which never took too much time.

Tea. Any flavor.

The brewing pot waterfalled orange jasmine tea into a cast-iron cup with no handle.

_____ sipped and took a seat when gestured to do so by the emaciated debtor.

Recently shaved palm trees stretched their trunks outside in the balmy air like over-groomed poodles. The two of them gazed through the windows as if that was what they'd come there to do.

I'll lose my citizenship after this, the debtor said after several minutes of presumably enjoying his beverage in silence some feet away from a rather deadly and precise agent of the Nation.

_____ hummed, a D-sharp, a low, pensive note, not without pity but

certainly not without resolve. And then
something happened, a tightening of
_____'s trachea, a slight but
sudden increase in heart rate, and for
the first time _____ took her
eyes away from the skyline and moved them
to the debtor's, milky blue lenses in a
mildly perspiring skeletal face.

*Wouldn't it be terrible for someone to
go through that?* he asked. *To lose everything for a few incomplete transactions.
I have a family. My daughter isn't very
smart, not like you. She's not capable of
earning citizenship. Did you earn yours?*

Inherited, _____ said through a
dry cough.

That single word alarmed _____,
as much as we can ascertain alarm from
this vantage point. It was certainly more
personal information than she'd ever di-
vulged to a debtor in all her years of
service to the Nation. A hand went to her
throat as the cough persisted.

Please, just let me start over, the
debtor continued as _____'s cough
became much more violent. She pushed
her teacup to the edge of the desk, just
short of surrendering it to gravity. The
debtor put his wrist out to _____
and she lifted a finger from the edge of
the desk. She held on desperately to the
desk's edge, to regain her breath and com-

posure. A fever erupted and _____
fell to her knees.

Shit, he whispered. Though soundproof,
his office remained transparent, as several eyes noticed the visiting agent col-
lapse onto her hands and knees. *You cannot
die here. Get up, okay. Please*, he begged,
shoving his wrist under _____'s
face, a few ropes of her hair loosened
from the thunderous coughing.

_____ pulled herself to her
feet with a ragged, moist breath and teary
eyes before coughing one last time, sending a projectile of mucus onto the surface of the desk. In the wad of phlegm,
_____ could see fragments of
some orange foreign substance. The fever
broke, the coughing ceased. She drew her
weapon and aimed it at the debtor's left
eye. He blinked a lash across the barrel
before falling to the floor with a finger
extended. _____ waved her wrist
near the digit and told him thank you.

_____ could not directly remember the last time she had become so ill,
and based on her elevated blood pressure,
adrenaline levels, and disregard for auto-
mobile speeds as she crossed intersections
to the trains back to the Corp. headquar-
ters, she was concerned. Several sections
of the Corporation were (rarely) used for

treatment of illness or injury but were designated for health services. The facilities were research laboratories and maintenance stations to monitor particular technological configurations applied to high-ranking officials. _____ arrived at a familiar wing.

Anemone, she whispered after entering through the glass door.

Anemone did not hear the statement, because the auditory volume on her listening device blocked any outside noise. Anemone improvised what some but not all would call a dance while humming over several vials of fluid.

Anemone, _____ said a little louder to no effect.

While glancing around through the transparent walls for anyone else and finding no one, _____ reached over and grabbed Anemone by the shoulders and spun her around. Anemone screamed, then removed her listening tab from her ear.

What the shit, _____?

Anemone . . .

I have quantum diadems in sequence over here! This is revolutionary shit, not that the Corp. will give a damn, unless I figure out how to commodify or weaponize them, which I will (maybe) if I feel like it. The heads will love it as always. I could pitch my left ass cheek into the boardroom and they'd faint from glee. Imagination is not their greatest gift. You look terrible, dearest.

Anemone removed her gloves and took _____'s face in her hands.

Love this, though. Now the uniform department, genius. Your eyes, though. Is this a salinated secretion? Have you been crying?! Anemone was almost delighted at the novelty.

I am sick, _____ admitted in a nearly embarrassed whisper.

Impossible, Anemone said, giggling.

She was a mutant, we suspect. Her parents were premier geneticists of the era, responsible for perfecting and legalizing human cloning and then erecting every possible law against the procedure soon after. They were more like architects than scientists in the end, designing new and more efficient ways to stack the genes of humankind with remarkable if not terrifying outcomes, their own daughter one of those incredible results, one that they'd lamented secretly in journals discovered posthumously. Anemone earned four advanced degrees before puberty and occupied the most varied of roles in the Corporation, mostly at her own discretion. Her propensity for academic excellence had made her invaluable though rather lonely until later in her adult life, when she

discovered an affinity for sexual stimulation while consuming sugary foods. She
made many friends then.

Dearest dear, sit. Sit! Anemone ordered.

_____ obliged, in a position of
defeat.

Will I be decommissioned?

You sound almost hopeful. What a crime.
Anemone smiled, then abandoned the effort
for supplication.

_____ pulled out a piece of
tissue with the residue of snot and orange fragments that had emerged violently
earlier.

Oh! Anemone exclaimed.

It was the *oh* of uninhibited delight, a
gift, a mystery, a jewel, a snack, perhaps.
Anemone did not eat the item; however, she
slid it onto an illuminated dock, then
touched a switch. Anemone retrieved a
small wand from a drawer nearby.

Uncross   your   legs,   she   ordered
_____.

Anemone crouched and ran the wand along
the biometric seam of _____'s leg-
wear while meeting her eyes. The light of
the wand changed gently from a warm white
to green. Some centuries before, green
had become the color of safety and balance. She placed a hand on _____'s
right knee for balance and probably something else, an inability to resist contact

with something physically attractive, like passing a flower on the street. Humans do this with soft textures, warm surfaces, symmetrical structures, bodies of all kinds, whether stingrays or breasts. They must touch what they admire even as that admiration transforms into something more consuming and destructive, like hunger.

Anemone stood and hummed contentedly at the green glow of the wand, then turned to the data port as it concluded the analysis of the sample.

Oh, she said.

Oh? _____ repeated.

Oh, Anemone said in a lower tone, brows heavy.

Oh!

Oh.

Anemone!

You are not sick, dear. You're in premier condition, thanks to my exemplary care.

Anemone, please.

Dear, you are not sick. It is poison!

Anemone laughed, the most sincere laugh, a slap-on-her-thigh laugh, as if the world could not be more ridiculous than at that moment. Then the laugh turned to a more serious smile.

Killing the poor fool is all that must be done now. So much failure for one person in a day. It's something, isn't it.

What kind of poison?

It looks to have primarily neurological effects. If I must guess, it should be calming.

I do not feel calm.

Anemone laughed again.

Dear, of course not on you. Your bio nodes are second to none. They recognize toxins immediately and proceed to gather and expel them. The process is a little uncomfortable, though.

Anemone rubbed the remaining dried tears from _____'s eyes.

But, yes, on an ordinary body—that of a noncitizen, certainly—the effect would be tranquility, compliance, suggestibility, and . . .

And what?

The system recognizes this formula in the criminal enforcement records. There is a narcotics classification. It's cute. They're such poets in narcotics. Mercy for suicide. Nostalgia for . . . well, let's not state the obvious, so much fun in drugs.

Anemone.

They call this one Forgiveness.

SUNDAY

When Coral began an unyielding obsession with Khadija's mother, Naima, they were juniors in high school.
Compton in the 1990s was a mecca, an Eden, a place to
dream, honor; to buy liquor, doughnuts, fried chicken
and greens; a place to loathe and protect; a fantasy and
a nightmare. Residents were mostly Black, brown, and
working-class. Covenants between the city and the people were signed at birth, a deal struck to give back to the
land if the land let them go. Promises were not often kept.
Stars came out of Compton: athletes and artists. Most
just ran and never returned, but when the city let someone
leave, they left with gifts.

In the Clinic for Accidentally Killing the Person You Only
Meant to Seduce, we are seventeen years old with a crush
on one of our brother's girlfriends. These situations end
one way or another; someone always dies. The girlfriends
mine us for information. They are jealous. They are beautiful. They wear jewelry in perfect balance and have no
acne. They smell like sweet chemicals.

Naima could do hair and made money doing it. She wore
Nike Cortez sneakers, a different color for every day of

the week, all paid for with braiding money. Coral asked Naima to braid her hair on a Saturday while Jay played basketball in the park. Teen years are different from other periods of time. Naima was older than Jay the way Coral was older than Jay, and for some reason that was strange. It also seemed strange to Coral that Jay was fifteen with bad grades and bad breath but already dating three girls.

In the Clinic for Accidentally Killing the Person You Only Meant to Seduce, we pay close attention to our hair. Hair is power. Hair climbs into the subconscious and evokes weakness or the ability to navigate difficult situations.

Where Coral was tall, hard, relatively linear, and dour, Naima was shorter, soft, curved, and smiling. Naima wanted to please her.

I got everything you told me to from the shop, Coral said. *How much do you charge?*

This looks good.

Naima peeked into the black plastic bag full of synthetic hair and gel.

How long will it take?

A few hours.

Okay, cool.

An intimate bond developed when people touched each other's hair and scalps, a distinct release of pleasure hormones. So when Naima slid the ponytail holder from Coral's head and pressed her fingernails to Coral's scalp, they both sighed in a special kind of ecstasy. They were strangers before the touch, then abruptly something else.

Coral began to wonder what Jay and Naima did when they were together, something Coral had never really witnessed. His girlfriends were abstractions, ideas of girls, often stupid and hollow, like a cartoon with no sound. Naima was warm and had a cute smile.

What do you even see in Jay?

Naima laughed.

She had started braiding from the base of Coral's head and worked upward. The scalp was parted into squares, slicked with gel before attaching the long strands of synthetic hair in a knot that Coral considered magical because it was beyond her ability to reproduce it. Naima draped a finished braid over Coral's collar.

How about that length?

Longer.

Waist?

Yup.

He's nice when his friends aren't watching too close.

He's also twelve.

He's not! He's fifteen, almost sixteen.

It's weird.

It's not!

Almost weird.

Coral, stop.

Ugh. Why are boys so dumb?

Right. Just be a person.

Not some team of bozos. You can't date one bozo. You have to date 'em all.

You're funny. Jay said you crack jokes a lot.

Ew, he talks about me? I mean, I am remarkable.

Naima laughed again.

What does he say about me? Naima asked.

In the Clinic for Accidentally Killing the Person You Only Meant to Seduce, we hurt feelings by accident through compliments that feel like judgments. You look nice today. You've done something to your hair. Have you lost weight? We are dentists in brightly colored offices meant for children, reciting a phrase over and over like a prayer: *This will only sting a little.* We say too much and watch the light go out of our lovers like the yolk of the sun disappearing over the sea. They are strangled. They are beheaded. They are insulted. They are lost to us.

I haven't heard much.

Oh.

Nine hours later, Coral felt undone. Naima had gone quiet for a long time. During the breaks Coral had a chance to check on the progress, to observe the transformation in herself, the short puff of hair spiraling out into shining ropes, the incongruity of it all, like a gosling, uncanny, awkward, and endearing. She wanted to tell Naima all of what Jay had actually said about her, how nothing was actually cruel and dismissive, how she was one of many, how Jay was young, foolish, and mimicking a reckless, shortsighted kind of manhood easy to market in the hip-hop genre. He was simple and mean. Coral didn't know Naima really except for her touch, and that alone suggested she didn't deserve simple and mean.

Californians walked like they were underwater, slow, with all the time in the universe. Compton was a suburb of Los Angeles County, known for gangs, political corruption, and rap. Even time moved like water there, a thing to drown in, a thing necessary for life. Dreams would float or sink. The threat of violence from friends, from enemies, from strangers, from police, was constant, so constant that it became invisible, a kind of white noise.

Coral didn't have language for herself yet, for how she would love and walk through the world. Jay owned a twenty-seven-by-forty-inch *Poetic Justice* movie poster, framed above his bed, the iconic Janet Jackson with box braids cascading over her shoulder, her gaze aimed at the adjacent blank white wall. When Naima finished the braids, she draped the final one over Coral's right shoulder like Janet's.

We just need to seal the tips in hot water.

That meant heating the plastic hair to the point where it fused and would not unravel. Coral stood up and went to the nearest reflective surface, which was the microwave. Naima smiled at her while screwing a tub of gel closed. The weight of the braids made Coral lean and sway for control of her body in a manner that was unequivocally feminine. She approved. Coral nodded at Naima in a gesture more posh than peer. Naima shook her head and laughed.

You are silly.

In a brief moment Coral recognized something finite and wondrous, the temporary condition of youth, beauty, the space between death and the fear of not living, how fragile and perfect a second can be before shattering unceremoniously into oblivion: Naima full of light.

Eight thousand or so days later, Coral was alone. Two days after her brother's suicide, Coral needed eggs. Eggs are one of a few objects that made people (in America, mostly) believe in God. They are perfect. She opened and closed Jay's refrigerator on Sunday at 7:07 a.m. Two minutes later she repeated the action. Nothing inside the refrigerator had changed. A particular vision of the typical American breakfast could not manifest based on the ingredients at hand. In her own home she possessed flour, baking powder, salt, sugar, butter, milk, oil, and, yes, eggs. She could've made pancakes or waffles. She might've had some overripe blueberries lingering and some cardamom to spice up the meal. Jay also did not own flour or baking powder.

Coral entered the grocery store with the gait and demeanor of a surgeon who'd lost her last patient in the operating room and was determined not to fuck up again. The typical grocery store had lighting similar to hospital lighting, but every other sensory experience varied. The chill of the dairy aisle repulsed Coral, so she found herself standing before the wall of cereals unique to the United States in its sheer vastness and variety. An array of cartoon figures posed jovially on each box—a tiger, a pirate, a chipmunk, a vampire, a caveman, a frog, Black athletes. Coral knew she wasn't supposed to be there. Sugar was not the objective. Coral wanted to smell the pancakes more than consume them. A woman pushing a shopping cart with a noisy child of six years or so walked behind her. The child carried a carton of macaroni and cheese in each hand and shook them like maracas.

In the Clinic for Accidentally Killing the Person You Only Meant to Seduce, we give bad directions to hikers we pass on mountain trails, to food delivery drivers, to patients in the emergency room, to colleagues who want our sweet potato pie recipe. We want to be the best at what we do and forget that means nothing without an audience. We cook breakfast on summer mornings for our little brother. He is ten and we are twelve and we are king. He watches in his boy body, a thing not yet a threat and still vibrating with danger and a fascination with fire. He asks us what goes in the pancake mix. We say, *White stuff.* He says, *Salt?* We say, *Yes, mostly salt.* He nods and we smile in our cruelty.

Eggs: the Species needed to eat during stages of crisis and euphoria. Not long after More was discovered and put to great and terrible use across the ages, eventually the Species recognized Investment. Some things acquired could multiply over time. We believe they were aware of this since birth. An investment, however, did not exactly duplicate itself but provided something in addition to itself, i.e., the egg. Our records are not clear, but we believe that before the Species lived a long time, they lived a very short time, and before that a very, very long time, around when the toxins of the planet were thin and violence against themselves was not yet perfected. We also theorize that chickens were very large and needed to be restrained with ropes and pulleys and produced yolks substantial enough to drown pets. We think. We know the egg became treasure and waste and a measure of economic success for the duration of the Species' existence. The egg provided a nearly ideal protein-to-fat ratio with minimal side effects for the body. We have studied the shape, the density, the shell, all of which are nothing short of a Fibonacci-scale genius manifested, a sign of the divine, or of the universe showing off. So many mistakes occur in the painful process of evolution and adaptation to the changing states of environments, but when a solution as beautiful as the egg presents itself, all life must sing hallelujah.

Every carton contained a crack. Coral had freed herself from the cereal aisle to the tundra that was the wall of dairy cages. She stood in the refrigerated section with the glass door propped against her shoulder while she opened every carton of eggs, one at a time. Nothing pure. Nothing safe. Over and over again. The first carton seemed fine until the thin membrane of loose whites slid across her fingertips; the crack was hidden. The eighth carton looked like it had been smashed by a jug of milk. Coral checked it anyway, the desperation running uninhibited in her veins. A nightmare lay inside.

Can I help you with anything?

A store attendant smiled at Coral, a handsome-young-man smile, bright teeth and evil-villain mustache, racially vague enough to put in a commercial. He was taller than Coral by half a foot.

In the Clinic for Accidentally Killing the Person You Only Meant to Seduce, we are grandparents at church Christmas pageants. When our granddaughter finishes her imitation of Mary and is proud, we walk up to her and say, *There is a stain on your shirt*, and nothing else. We check our watches and discuss buffet options at Sizzler.

Jay's phone vibrated.

Summer: Youve been quiet. Are we still meeting Thursday

Summer: I'll come over today since you're off

In the Clinic for Accidentally Killing the Person You Only Meant to Seduce, we are best friends to girls with little imagination. They are pretty and used to seeing money move around with little consequence to themselves. We are acquiescent in a world designed to commodify our existence like olives turned to oil. They admire us and want to know what they should like and not like. They are not very smart, but they are kind and easy to amuse. We promise to take them on vacations when we are famous. We plan road trips to the Grand Canyon. We imagine our weddings and homes and living in cities with spectacular public transportation infrastructure. We get better jobs than expected, in cities with decent public transportation, and leave those best friends behind. We tell them they are a flight away and we will always be there for them. We get promoted. We buy rental properties. We forget their whole names.

Coral wanted to hear the eggs mixing into batter, the slow smack of wet and dry.

Sometimes we do the swap trick. Can I show you?

Coral surrendered the carton of eggs she held out to the young man. He smiled and began taking out the clean whole eggs and setting them on the side of the shelf. He opened another carton and began taking the gently cracked eggs out and putting them into the other carton.

After making space, he put all the good eggs together in one carton and handed them to Coral.

My mom taught me that.

He smiled again, lovely and sincere. Coral smashed the eggs.

Eggs, the future: the egg of five thousand years ago and the egg of today are not much different, we estimate.

In the Clinic for Accidentally Killing the Person You Only Meant to Seduce, we are almost finished making pancakes for ourselves and our little brother when he pours salt into the batter while we are looking for a spatula. We scream at him and take the salt carton away with a violence we had not needed ever before. His eyes water and he says he wanted to help. We want to cry. We laugh and we are hungry.

In the Walmart parking lot off Fifth Street, Coral pretended to be her dead brother via texts with a stranger named Summer. It was a seventy-eight-degree morning. This part of Long Beach remained bifurcated: the upper view blue skies and tops of palm trees, the lower view shadowy concrete littered with garbage that suggested high levels of desperation, such as overfull diapers, fast-food wrappers, vomit, and losing lottery tickets. Summer had no face to Coral, no smell, no past, no ambition, or anyone else that knew her or loved her. Most humans afforded other humans common courtesies such as not telling them how horrible their day really had been or that they found each other's appearance disturbing. More often than not they pretended to be or think as someone other than themselves to avoid sudden, unpredictable emotions like anger, fear, or disappointment. This was a mistake.

Summer: how fun?

Jay: however fun you want lol

Summer: Morongo fun?

Jay: sure

Summer: Im not joking

Jay: me either. Morongo Thursday

Summer: You don't work Thursday now

Jay: I have days I can take

Summer: something is wrong lol you trying to not work

Jay: lol

Summer: Im smiling like a idiot at the desk right now my super-visor is eyeballing

Jay: lmao

Coral did not acquire the food she'd set out for, and the hunger bit hard at her center despite the distraction of chatting with someone so excited. She started her car and drove onto the avenue. Pedestrians in two modes of existence, conscious and beyond consciousness, walked, leaned and lingered at the bus stops, exited stores, pushed their carts of clothes to the Laundromat on the corner. None smiled.

Jay: you know me. I take care of my girl

Summer: . . .

Summer: something like that :)

In the Clinic for Accidentally Killing the Person You Only Meant to Seduce, we are a sophomore in college at our father's home taking pictures of our little brother as he prepares for prom. He is in a rental suit with a silver vest and handkerchief. His date, Naima, is in a silver dress like mercury. She belongs on a coin, bright and immortal, we think. Our little brother poses and smiles but is unhappy, does not like his date, and puts his arm around her only when a camera lifts, then immediately removes it. We know Naima is pregnant. We don't mention it to our mother or our aunts until they mutter with suspicion. We confirm with a nod and say nothing. We know Naima can hear and we continue. She smiles for the flash of the camera again and again.

When hunger stops it is time to worry or it is time to think of nothing at all, because the pain of living is over. Coral's hunger suddenly disappeared like a stain wiped from a counter. She could remember the sensation without actually finding it with her nerves. Coral gripped the steering wheel of her vehicle with some force to assure herself that she was still real, in a world of tangible objects. The hunger felt like something to get back, the way old men used to try to find arousal by any means, a memory of something glorious now lost to the flesh. Coral imagined pancakes again, bad ones she ate as a child, tight and dense with sticky syrup full of artificial flavors. The hunger flickered like dead flint.

In the Clinic for Accidentally Killing the Person You Only Meant to Seduce, we are wealthy and we are bored. We look for ways to spend our money that make other people move as we wish. We run for Congress. We own companies. We make promises. We believe our own words and forget we have bodies. We believe we are cerebral even though our armpits have odor and our faces age and shed skin cells and we lose teeth. We wear outrageously expensive clothing and perfume because we need inaccessible barriers between ourselves and the people we want to control.

Coral parks in front of Jay's apartment, which is unchanged from when she left. The more she tried to jumpstart her hunger with memories of pleasant eating, the more the sensation flickered from desire to nausea. She abandoned the effort altogether in exchange for acceptance that this was the price of the hour.

We do not understand self-manufactured suffering as much as we study the concept. We begin as good researchers always begin, with compelling points of inquiry: Why did humans cause so much unnecessary pain? Obligation? Jealousy? Competition? Shame? Our answers are complex formulas that we recite as law.

Jay: see you soon

Coral and Jay attended Khadija's elementary school end-of-year awards ceremony, where Naima was rumored to potentially be in attendance. Most of the other students there had a mother guaranteed to be present, but certainly not all. Some mothers were working and a few were dead. Naima had been lost to depression and a Vicodin addiction for years. Mothers like this became more than women: they became myths. To Coral, Compton often felt haunted on days like that one, a late-spring evening warm in the fading sunlight and cold in the shade, walking into a building she hadn't seen inside since she was a child herself, waiting for strangers or monsters to appear. Some parents brought gifts, stuffed animals and balloons, to which Jay said, *It's not a fucking graduation.* Coral nodded enthusiastically, both their bank accounts feeling the bite of a recession and skeptical even about going out for burgers after.

Coral swiveled her head around the auditorium once she was seated, scanning for potential glimpses of Naima. She expected to see the Naima of old, shimmering with a soft touch, wide eyes full of patience and kindness. She saw only other families, plump women years younger than their faces and a few men in T-shirts, with strong arms and shoulders, all tired, very tired. Khadija sat with her peers in the rows near the stage. Jay's policy was not to talk about Naima, which added to her mystique. Coral wondered what Khadija thought of a woman she'd rarely seen after age three. Did she consider Naima at all? Did she feel her absence with so many cousins and aunts? Did she worry about her mother's safety? Did she know women were not always safe in that world? Did she hope her mother suffered for making her suffer? A teacher in a blue blazer with extraordinarily large buttons shaped like the heads of lions took the podium and began issuing certificates of various achievements. The auditorium door opened and Coral turned quickly to see who had entered. A man, no one to her.

In the Clinic for Accidentally Killing the Person You Only Meant to Seduce, we are in a park with our daughter. She is nine years old. We have nursed many addictions longer than we have nursed our child. We have lost custody and this is a scheduled visit. The park is empty apart from aggressive squirrels and chatty birds. The grass has not gotten enough water. Everything is dry and hard and we tell our daughter to stop lying about us. She is silent. We tell our daughter that we are trying our best and that her father is cruel and has always been that way. She is silent. We strike her. We strike her hard in her chest to make words come out. This is what our daughter says to the judge. Everyone believes our daughter.

The last of the awards are called. These are the biggest prizes, tiny plastic trophies for good grades. The other awards, for vague and meaningless things like citizenship and camaraderie, seem more vague and meaningless than ever. Khadija walks to the stage to receive her fourth award of the evening as Jay and Coral applaud and her friends scream in support. Coral checks again for any- one else standing. She's memorized the crowd, the mus- taches and the wigs. They are all no one, and then the door opens again, someone is leaving, a woman, a husk, a ghost of someone Coral knew: Naima in the dark. Coral sighs in relief, then clenches in frustration. She will tell no one. She has no one to tell.

We often think about the heart, the meat and the metaphor, how the idea of life centered around that mus- cle, how they learned to keep it going and how to make it stop when they wanted. Jay thought mostly about money, how little he had and how hard it was to keep any and how little he had to keep. He cooked for Khadija and bought some of the things she was brave enough to ask for, like shoes. He named her after the Prophet Muham- mad's wife and a nineties sitcom character. He was proud and a little flippant. He would become angry when things were out of his control, and he didn't have the language, like Coral did, to be clear and specific about his feelings. Coral had much more to say but knew the words had to stay locked inside with no way to shake them free.

All three of them ate burgers and shared fries at Tam's Burgers, while Khadija held her trophy and certificates in her lap.

The thing known as the Internet lost its imagination and cannibalized itself.

2021 SUNDAY 1:05 P.M.

TOP STORIES

DEPARTMENT OF JUSTICE PROBE INTO MALL SHOOTER'S PARENTS STILL UNDERWAY

Smithsburg, Md. Police say a mix of legal and illegal firearms was easily accessible in the suspect's parents' home when it was searched after the shooting that killed fourteen and injured more than a dozen.

NEW EVIDENCE DISCOVERED AFTER TESTIMONY FROM TEACHERS AND WITNESSES ABOUT THE FAMILY'S ODD BEHAVIOR OVER COURSE OF A YEAR

NINE-YEAR-OLD MASS-SHOOTING SURVIVOR TESTIFIES BEFORE CONGRESS: "HELP IT NOT HAPPEN AGAIN"

FORMER PRESIDENT AND FAMILY CONTINUE TO DELAY COURT HEARING

A GENERATION OF MEN DON'T WANT TO HAVE SEX AND ARE WILLING TO KILL FOR THAT TO BE OKAY

They were known once as incels, a derogatory term turned mark of pride for young men, mostly of European ancestry, who degrade women with such fury that to desire them sexually becomes repulsive. The hate stemmed from various theories: from simple rejection to a patriarchal world that so devalued femininity that it corrupted a common-sense appreciation of gender diversity.

We know that the movement, a search for belonging and

understanding, began in the bedrooms of young men, ordinary, solitary, musky lairs where youths felt safe in their feelings. These young men brooded in their private spaces, presumably in comfortable homes. Whether they had two parents, one, or none at all, they were invisible in those spaces, in the towns and cities they roamed, unnoticed by their peers or by women, unremarkable in their achievements, and desperate for a way to climb out of their mediocrity. In chat rooms these young men discovered they were not alone in this revelation. The digital community provided the warmth of companionship unfamiliar to these men, and they flourished within them, developing their own language for their identity, a kind of currency for their hatred, and ultimately a nation to which they could pledge their citizenship.

Zacharias Jones, who identified as an incel, recently killed his former next-door neighbor, his best friend, and then himself. Jones's first victim was Vanessa Wright, who lived across the street from the Jones residence between 2005 and 2013. Jones killed Vanessa seven years after she moved away; she was engaged and had a one-year-old son. "I'd never seen him before in my life," the fiancé told the police. "He was nobody."

We know that the power of the computer amplified the reach of these men and their deeply buried disregard for anything not traditionally classified as "male." They became a family. Everything outside that family became incidental or a threat. Women in the concrete reality were their mothers and sisters and neighbors, with heads of hair and hobbies and incomes and reasons to leave the house and commitments to see to completion. Women in the abstract were senators and celebrities and high school crushes. They were profile pictures sending out messages that challenged a philosophy based on gender hierarchy. They were enemies and casualties in a war of the incel's own imagination. Women in the incel's fantasy vision of the world were things to be traded like Pokémon cards, assigned value by men, and owned by men.

When these young men tried to live in the real world with old rules and a population of women consistently and miraculously greater than men, they were met with cruelty and dismissal even by other men. In a court statement, the brother of Jones's best friend recounted, "Zach told me it was gay to have sex with women. I laughed then. I'm not laughing now." Jones was sentenced to thirty years and was found dead from asphyxiation in his cell.

Whereas Jones was one individual, the movement is in the millions. The logic of their religion could not hold up, and again they were threatened with oblivion.

FIVE BRITISH ROYALS RUN INTO PERILOUS STUMBLING BLOCK AS ERA OF NEW PARLIAMENT BEGINS

SF POP-UP FUSION RESTAURANTS ARE BECOMING A NIGHTMARE FOR THE UNHOUSED

SF MAYOR'S TESLA DOUSED IN PINK SLUSHY BOMBING BY DISGRUNTLED CONSTITUENT

THE RICHEST MEN IN THE WORLD ALL AGREE ON THIS ONE STRATEGY FOR MAXIMUM INVESTMENT RETURNS

WHAT PAST MARKETS SAY WORKS BEST TO RIDE OUT A BEAR MARKET

HOMEOWNERS ARE DOING THIS TO PUT EQUITY
TO PROPER USE

BILLIONAIRE CELEBRITY ACCUSED OF FUNDING
NEWS ORGANIZATIONS IN ORDER TO PLANT
SELF-PROMOTING ARTICLES THAT BOOST HIS
COMPANIES' STOCK VALUE

FOR YOU IN THE NEWS

BUZZFEED'S 10 TIMES PARENTS KNEW THEIR
CHILDREN WERE DISAPPOINTMENTS AND NO ONE
ELSE BUT THE PARENTS WERE TO BLAME

THIS COMMON ANTI-AGING PROCEDURE RUINED
MY LIFE: I SUED AND THE JUDGE HAD THIS TO SAY

BEST SEX POSITION FOR OPTIMAL PLEASURE FELL
OUT OF FASHION BUT IS BACK TO ACCLAIM

THE CHILD-FREE MOVEMENT AMONG MILLENNIAL
WOMEN IS BLAMED FOR RISE IN
ANTIDEPRESSANT PRESCRIPTIONS

Wellness boutiques, yoga boot camps, luxury vacations—all
are staples of the modern guide to a life well lived for women
in the millennial generation, provided they don't have any
kids. Another staple of millennial womanhood appears to be a
robust supply of Zoloft and other prescription antidepressants,
according to a privately funded study out of Wayne University.
The findings established a correspondence between not having children and taking happy drugs.

   "What a depressing argument," Toni Sawyer wrote in her

blog, *Child-Free and Blessed*, a chronicle of a life lived will-fully without children. Sawyer is a self-proclaimed "lucky baby ducky" who lives off a trust in Miami with her partner, Tim Thompson. Both are adamantly against marriage, homeown-ership, and, of course, having kids. Sawyer has been a vocal opponent of the data published from the study since the mo-ment she learned of it. "Horrendous anti-woman propaganda," she calls it. "Take a look around. Women might be depressed and in greater need of therapies right now, but it certainly isn't because they aren't having enough babies."

Sawyer certainly has a point when considering the over-all happiness scale of the nation compared to those of other first-world countries. Scarcity, economic decline and uncer-tainty, governmental instability, job losses, and environmental catastrophe are not in short supply around the globe. The inter-section of these crises could very well be a contributing factor, according to Sawyer and her supporters. Over two hundred thousand subscribers follow Sawyer's affirmations about life as a "child-free" woman and what Sawyer calls "unburdening women from the archaic gendered pressures to care for some-one other than themselves." Children or not, general happiness is down overall across every demographic measured. So, too, is the birth rate.

Sawyer's popular blog is not without its dissenters, who post regular contradictory and often hostile rebuttals to Sawyer's points about the link between happiness and not having chil-dren. "I love my kids," writes Melissa X, who wished to use only her first name to protect her identity. "She's telling me I would be happier without them. Being a mother is hard. It's the hard-est and lowest-paying job there is. It's also the most important. Without mothers we would let kids suffer hopelessly. And now we have evidence that women are poisoning their bodies to feel better just because they refuse to do the natural and beautiful thing they were designed for. That woman should be ashamed, and I'll tell her every day of my life if I have to." That kind of language might not be what her attorney wants on the record, considering that the trial date for Melissa's alleged vandalism of Sawyer's property is looming.

"She put diapers every f***ing where. They were taped to my car, in the wheel well, all the windows. They're all nuts," Sawyer says, laughing, from her beach condo. "I welcome their input, though. They're worried about a lot of legitimate things: their communities, the future, and their own place in it. It can be terrifying to wake up and not have a purpose, or to confront the idea that your assigned purpose might be a scam. I've been there more than once. Those are dark days, and some of us need a pill to get through them. But it makes no sense to argue that the solution is to be responsible for the care of another generation that is being thrown over and over again into the same sad set of rules, and I have a feeling, based on my feedback, that it makes no sense to a lot of people. As for the naysayers, at least they're considering something other than what they're used to."

CLIMATE WORRY SPARKS NEW WAVE OF UNCONTROLLED ANXIETY AMONG GEN ZS, AS IT SHOULD

EXPERTS SAY TO EXPECT WILDFIRE SEASON TO BE HARSHEST EVER RECORDED

Wildfires in the Pacific Northwest have become a common seasonal occurrence, but they are happening in increasingly unlikely locales. I met with Arizona forest management ranger Mitchell Bradshaw, who prefers to go by Mitch, on a bright April day. By all normal accounts the temperature was perfect. The air quality was good. It was a beautiful morning but by most people's accounts Mitch looked grim. "I've never seen anything like it," Mitch said, gazing mournfully into the dry riverbed in Snakehead State Park. That seems to be a phrase heard often in the area and in more and more environments across the world.

Mitch is 5'2", with forearms more massive than my own calves, and I'm 6'1", not known to skip leg day. When I said that he reminded me of a cartoon character, he looked at me with complete seriousness and said, "I don't watch television. It'll make you stupid." Noted. I needed Mitch to trust that what he was telling me would be treated with care. I needed Mitch's institutional knowledge. I needed Mitch to not knock me on my ass and leave me in the desert two days before my birthday. After a gorgeous hike up the mountain and down into the basin where the rivers connect with other rivers, Mitch showed me lines in the rock. "It used to be here. Now it's there." Mitch pointed to the change in water levels visible to the eye from fifty feet away.

We walked another forty minutes to a different dry spot. "I used to swim in this part of the river. I called it a pond back then," Mitch said. There was no water, no pond, no river, just Mitch and his memories, and I hadn't cut my toenails as short as I'd needed to that morning, so my feet were starting to hurt. I knew before coming that there hadn't been a quality snowfall up north in over three years. Everything is tinder. Some would think that this is always the case in the desert, but the desert is actually juicy. There's water where it's supposed to be, if you know where to squeeze or dig. At least that used to be the case.

"What have we done?" I asked Mitch, and he laughed. I was being reverential. "You're one of those drama boys. Yeah, we're screwed, but it ain't the end, you know." I was offended. "What's the end then?" I asked him. Mitch didn't answer me, and I didn't expect him to. I threw the rock I was holding. I was being dramatic. Then I lost hold of whatever that feeling was that had me annoyed with Mitch and the state of the world as a whole. Maybe I do skip leg day every once in a while. Maybe Mitch didn't have any knowledge I desperately needed, after all. Maybe the whole point was

DISNEY'S NEW, MYSTERIOUS INTERACTIVE RIDE ON HOLD DUE TO UNFORESEEABLE EVENTS

YOU-KNOW-WHO WORE SOMETHING, POSTED SOMETHING, OR ATE SOMETHING, AND HERE IT IS

RECORD MOGUL CHARGED WITH DISAPPEARANCE OF EX-GIRLFRIEND IS ARRESTED IN BEVERLY HILLS

We note how often the Species folded in on itself in this way, the eating of its own body. The catalyst is always the same: the root of anger that turns to violence, mapped like the stars in our catalogs. We call it loneliness.

MONDAY

THE MONDAY FOLLOWING Coral's discovery of her brother's dead body, she went to work on what was supposed to be an exciting new step in her career, and whenever someone asked how she was doing she said, *I'm fine*, and smiled. Everyone seemed convinced and had no reason to think otherwise.

In the Clinic for Dying While Willfully Participating in a Poorly Thought-Out Cultural Trend and Becoming a Martyr for Revolution, we sit in a conference room and listen to a man speak. He stands up so we can see his body and leans over the table with both palms on the surface to emphasize the length of his limbs and his weight. The good idea for the day has already happened, and it came from someone else's mouth. It doesn't matter anymore. We are here now and we cannot leave.

Coral stared at the stack of napkins arranged at the center of the table like an altar.

This was a time when people had many jobs or one job that had no practical function in society. They were called CEOs, supervisors, and executives. Most of the useful people carried the title of assistant or, on occasion, associate. Coral was neither an executive nor an assistant. She preferred the title of creator, artist, one who sends a thing of visceral emotional impact into the world and is then rewarded for that service. On that day, during that meeting, Coral remembered that her dead brother had no social media footprint whatsoever. She decided to create one. We understand the impulse. We imagine often what the dead might've done, had they made different choices. We worship the ghosts of history, marvel at desiccated tombs, and play in their dust. Therefore, what Coral proceeded to do was completely and totally sane and justifiable. Profile picture: sunglasses, driver's-side window, her brother's first car, a 1979 Cutlass Supreme, a.k.a. big ol' piece of shit. Bio: *Just doin me.*

When something is lost so suddenly, irrevocably, and spectacularly, there is no clear order of events to follow, especially when considering grief.

The office was not chic or luxurious. It was a bungalow on a large concrete lot. The air conditioner did not always work. Coral enjoyed the space, usually. She enjoyed the other writers that shared the room with her, a blond woman too young and too clumsy to have a last name, who would be forever limited to Mel. Coral always brought napkins for the table in anticipation of some liquid cast haphazardly across the surface. Three men composed the remaining bodies, all in various states of alpha dominance competition. In a hundred years they would be required to eat one another, one leader at a time.

What do you feel like today? Mel asked Coral in a whisper.

I don't know.

Coral continued and did not whisper.

Something light. Maybe a salad with a deep-dish pizza for dressing.

Mel giggled. Coral did not want to eat at all. She didn't want to think of teeth and meat and her body expanding.

Okay, just a salad then.

Not pizza? Mel whispered even lower, almost pleading. Coral laughed.

Sure, pizza.

That does sound good.

One of the co–alpha males deviated from his devotion to the speaker leaning over the table. Everyone bends to hunger eventually. Lunch became the objective of the hour and the hour after that, and there would be no creativity that day, to Coral's deep relief. She followed the recommended pages on Jay's new account. Videos of classic cars and Black celebrities emerged like mischievous spirits trapped in the frames. They sparkled and danced.

Who do they think he is? Coral said aloud to Jay's phone.

Who? Mel asked.

In the Clinic for Dying While Willfully Participating in a Poorly Thought-Out Cultural Trend and Becoming a Martyr for Revolution, we are twenty, a closeted lesbian, a virgin, and a junior in college. We are gangly like a fawn suffering from mild malnutrition. We are also beautiful, starving, lonely, and plagued by obsessive compulsions. We sit in the back of classrooms and pretend to be disengaged. We hear everything. We watch a girl with short curly hair every day in our African American literature lecture. She wears striped leggings and it looks like everything she does is deliberate. We spray the bottoms of our sneakers with Lysol before entering our dorm room. We eat a spoonful of peanut butter after the last class of the day and masturbate to documentaries of deep-sea creatures. These are our rituals. This is our religion.

Coral did not count the number of times when the truth of her world nearly escaped her. We did. We could see the cracks in her bones, the acid building in her muscles, and could only sigh in wonder, in admiration.

I'll order the pizzas today, Coral said. *My treat.*

In the Clinic for Dying While Willfully Participating in a Poorly Thought-Out Cultural Trend and Becoming a Martyr for Revolution, the sound of the ocean is arousing. We live away from the beach but close enough to it that it is not romantic, just available. We click on advertisements when bored, and are led to porn.

Are we absolutely set on pizza? the standing man said.

We think his voice dropped just a little for effect, but Coral did not hold on to the sound for very long before reaching for her phone. The other males seemed panicked and torn between the thought of not having pizza and of going against the suggestion of something else.

Fuck it. Pizza.

Mm-hmmm.

Why do you have two phones?

You are tits-deep in my business today, Mel.

I'm sorry!

Be sorry—and pineapple, bitch?

Mel laughed.

Yes, please.

Coral nodded while staring at her phone as the others

shouted pizza toppings, even though she was not actually ordering anything. She was modifying Jay's profile. She followed herself, then Khadija. She needed more photos to add in order to look legitimate and not like an artificial bot account. Then she remembered most men's accounts looked like illegitimate bot accounts, for the purpose of watching activity online and not being watched. Her finger hovered over the Photos app. She had not invaded anyone's privacy in this way before, especially family. Anything could be there and she was afraid. She was afraid she would see Jay as just a man. He would have all the things men had, meaning pictures of his penis to throw like digital Frisbees to anyone he possessed sexual interest in.

The dick pic was an art form, a language.

Like all languages, it was often misunderstood and always changing.

Margherita with olives, got it, Coral said.

Coral spun her chair to face the wall and closed her eyes. The room suddenly existed only in scents: Mel's banana sunscreen; peppermint; a carpet-cleaning solution; dry-erase marker; the two-hundred-dollar unisex cologne trending that month; breath; five different hair products in various chemical combinations of shea butter/coconut/ rose oil/selenium sulfide; paint; cigarette smoke from a generation ago, thin as a spiderweb; salt water; rubber; grass; and blood.

In the Clinic for Dying While Willfully Participating in a Poorly Thought-Out Cultural Trend and Becoming a Martyr for Revolution, we watch a television series that ended twenty years prior. We watch it on repeat for seven years, every evening.

Mel began to tell Coral that her plantar fascia was injured from riding her skateboard. Mel was thirty-two and started riding last year. Coral listened and everything around her felt tight but soft and manageable. The world seemed no bigger than the box the group sat in, and Coral couldn't decide if this was everything she'd ever wanted or a sad mistake. We often call that feeling grace. However, it could've just been satisfaction, regret, or the early stages of appendicitis.

After forty minutes Coral realized she'd forgotten to order the pizza.

Jay's phone dinged: a notification from Khadija.

The Los Angeles County Superior Courthouse is a granite mega-block structure with three statues of men affixed above the entrance like gargantuan, Eurocentric action figures gazing down at the damned. Jay had filed for custody months before, and the court date had finally arrived. Coral, Jay, and Khadija entered shortly before Naima. She clinked from the sound of all her jewelry and various metal bits affixed to her large handbag.

In the Clinic for Dying While Willfully Participating in a Poorly Thought-Out Cultural Trend and Becoming a Martyr for Revolution, we practice online dating. Our options are simultaneously vast and few—a sheriff with a blurry photo and two sons, a swimmer with hair to the middle of her torso, fourteen women whose personalities/ occupations appear to be avid consumption of marijuana, three Brazilian models that are probably men from Fresno, and all the others.

At the custody hearing for Khadija, the judge was the honorable Javier Cristobal, a tired man old as Coral and Jay's father, who had heard too many stories too many years ago to really believe in anything resembling justice. Naima wanted Khadija. A great decision had to be made and Judge Cristobal knew the risks that came with that decision, a life going in one direction over another, on his word. The machinations of the legal system at this time for the Species were tumultuous at best; highly subjective, biased, and mercurial on average; and at worst a vehicle for chaos and great suffering. The same can be said of online dating. Coral scrolled and clicked through the options after being filtered down like applications for a fast-food worker. She selected the sheriff for her first date and was stood up at La Vaquita, so she ordered two margaritas at the bar and watched the Wimbledon women's semifinals in true lesbian glory.

The statues on the front of the courthouse represented Mosaic law, the Magna Carta, and the Declaration of Independence. The first figure wore robes and a tablet, the middle one wore chain mail and carried the sword of a British knight and a scroll unfurled, and the last wore the high-collared cape and buckled boots of a seventeenth-century colonial American landowner with a rolled document tucked against his shoulder. The lawyers in Khadija's custody hearing were young white women in gray pencil skirts. Jay's lawyer presented a slideshow of images she'd collected from him. They were all of Khadija at amusement parks, birthday parties, school performances, duck ponds, and on Easter and Halloween. The seasons flashed by like pages turned in a book. The room was old but not graced with the theater of many other old rooms. It was white with wood accents. The witness stand had no barrier between the person testifying and the court, just a chair on a platform. Khadija was instructed to sit on that chair and answer questions. She was small, always small, especially compared with the long bodies of Jay and Coral. Khadija seemed like someone else suddenly to Coral, a stranger with a strange story, wearing the shell of her nine-year-old niece. Khadija had been a mean baby, eyebrows always furrowed in concern. Khadija had her hair shining with product and the barrettes clicked as she moved her head from left to right. From the nose up she looked like Naima, compelling in an ancient, almost alien way.

My mom hit me in the chest and told me to give her my birthday money.

Naima protested, called her a liar in a shrill voice Coral had never heard before. She stood up and looked at Khadija, then said, *Why is she lying? Why, why, why, why, why?* she asked again and again as if to a stranger. The bailiff restrained her. The judge brought his gavel down in two sharp strokes. It seemed an unreasonable and absurd reaction to a reasonable question that had not occured to Coral until that moment.

Coral did not give up on dating after the first attempt with the sheriff. She had dated men before and they were easy, abundant, and always wanted more than she imagined was worth the effort. Her second date was with a deejay living in West Hollywood. When Coral met her and greeted her by name, the woman looked surprised, then laughed. She said, *My name isn't Nicole.* Coral thought she'd made a mistake, confused the faces and names that blurred together like smoke on her computer screen, but not-Nicole said, *I just use that to be incognito. I'm Ty,* and it rhymed with *lie* so Coral could not think of much else the rest of the evening. The next weekend Coral had a movie date with a nursing student who looked closer to ten than twenty. Coral still watched the film, mostly forgetting she wasn't alone.

Judge Cristobal reviewed the evidence given to him. He appeared to listen and did not move much during any of the testimonies or the outbursts from Naima and her declarations of unfairness. There was little talk of the meaning of family, or love, or why any of them were there at all. The decision was about who would leave together. Naima, and her song of metal chiming with every step, left the courtroom first by herself. Afterward, everyone else was instructed to exit, following the formality that the winning party departs after the loser.

Coral remembered Naima's expression after Khadija testified, Naima's eyes dark and wide apart, beading with tears, her ancient beauty quaking from anger, or maybe shame, or maybe disappointment, or maybe terror that the life she had envisioned and planned for would be written away by a strange man on an arbitrary summer morning. This is a thing children were taught during this time, the limits of destiny for women. More often than not, girls were told that their destiny belonged to a god and that men were closer to gods than they would ever be, so one should modify one's expectations according to such a circumstance. Despite the court procedure to avoid confrontation with opposing parties, Coral, Jay, and Khadija met Naima in the parking lot. Up close it was clear that Naima was high but not too high and not high enough. They would not keep her attention for long and the tears were not sinking back. Coral stayed quiet, unsure of her role in this moment, not the mother and still an unspoken guardian. Addiction stretches the tether between realities, and Naima was on her way to another reality but not there yet. She looked at her daughter, then at Coral and Jay, and then up at the sky, at the big old stone men and said, *Well, there you have it.*

In the Clinic for Dying While Willfully Participating in a Poorly Thought-Out Cultural Trend and Becoming a Martyr for Revolution, we go on our fourth date and she lives in another state and feels exotic but familiar, like an item on the backside of a menu seen a hundred times but never ordered. We eat deep-dish pizza with giardiniera peppers, and it is disgusting. We make her laugh and have sex five times a day, unimpressed because we assume this is normal. We assume this is why everyone does this thing we have been so long deprived of and ask for nothing else in this world.

In an act of insecurity after she was stood up, Coral told the sheriff her photo was blurry so she must have something to hide. It triggered a four-hundred-word text response of bitter attacks to which Coral did not respond, the revenge of verbal abandonment complete.

We wonder if the unnamable thing was present that day between Khadija and Naima, a thing that was not love but something else, taut as silk, and we wonder if it could have been severed. Coral remembered Naima pregnant, wider than the hallways in her parents' house. She knew Naima believed she had something then.

.   .   .

After forgetting to order pizza for the office, Coral recognized an element of human nature often suppressed by business-casual attire, expensive shoes, hair gel, and the pretense of civility: hunger made them violent. The men paced and spoke abruptly about electric vehicle charging stations. Mel fidgeted with her phone and made notes on a legal pad. Coral had a sharp, indubitable sense that they would all eat her soon. She needed to escape.

I'll be right back.

Easy. She was out of the building, just a trailer on an expansive studio lot. In the unbearable light of the sun radiating off the pavement, Coral retreated into memory. Khadija was not patient and wanted to hear from her father. Coral was uncertain what Khadija might do now and terrified of who Khadija would become. There was a moment many years prior when Coral learned that Khadija spoke in two voices. She had a baby voice, soft and kind and painfully tender. Then she had her more common voice, gruff, abrupt, sarcastic, and biting. There was no in-between. Coral considered actually ordering pizza for the group but had a hard time wrapping her mind around the concept of pizza at all. *What is it anyway?* She instead worked more on Jay's new profile. The athletic theme she was crafting seemed convincing and all too familiar. Someone Jay knew had already sent a message. Coral had to ignore that for the moment. She didn't want to reveal who Jay maybe was, so she chose something else: anime fanboy.

Coral again remembered the pizza, the duty she'd embraced to feed her colleagues, and looked at her phone, the food apps like windows into tiny restaurants. Coral tried briefly but couldn't care about two-for-one specials or attempting to remember what strange and malicious pizza toppings they all wanted. It all fell out of her mind and her hands like salt. She hadn't gone far from the office door and so she turned around and peeked back inside.

Pizza is on the way, she said, and closed the door.

The hunger would help them, she reasoned. Mel was not good at living well in any way and the others were still shadows of greater men. Hunger would make them hunt, stimulate their imaginations at best, remind them how uncomfortable living often is, at least. If anyone survived in the room it would be Mel, even though she ate too much sodium and food with red dye 40, didn't treat her nail fungus, and all her lovers chose lakes over showers. She didn't take proper care of her body, but she guarded the one she had.

When Khadija spoke in two voices for the first time, she was fifteen. She told a story to Jay and then to Coral in separate rooms. The story featured mistreatment by a store employee when Khadija had tried to purchase frozen yogurt. Both tellings evoked empathy and familiarity about the strangeness of human interactions even if copious amounts of sugar are involved. It was the lowering in volume and word choice that struck Coral. She could sound eight or thirty, weird. Who was this person? Did Jay know her this way? What reward came from such a performance? It is said that trauma lives in voices, the throat returns to the age of pain when triggered.

Jay did not watch animated shows as a late teen or adult, not because he thought himself too old but because of the uncanny effect of hearing human voices over pictures. He once told Coral that watching cartoons was like separating from his body and ascending through the ceiling and away. Coral laughed. He was very serious.

In the Clinic for Dying While Willfully Participating in a Poorly Thought-Out Cultural Trend and Becoming a Martyr for Revolution, we watch cartoons with paper puppets that look like the dead. They cringe and smile as we throw popcorn on their happy flat paper mouths. They don't ever dream of anything else.

When Coral mentioned Khadija's baby voice, Jay did not understand. She visited his apartment on a Thursday to go out for dinner, and he sat trying to pay bills on his laptop. He did not understand that either. His irritation grew, so Coral pressed on as older sisters will. He denied the two voices and any implied problems with such ferocity that Coral felt she'd been slapped. She said, *Okay then*.

We consider the rewards for having two voices, two mouths. Is one a lie? Are they both lies? A child is afforded care and patience where an adult is afforded respect and indifference. We believe all voices are permanent records of damage.

Coral made up a few lies to tell as she walked across the empty concrete lot between bungalows. She thought she might tell the group the order had been delivered to someone else and they'd sent a refund. That might trigger an end-of-day and they would all depart, everyone defeated except Coral, victorious in her deceit. She wanted to include a robbery in the story somehow but knew Mel would be suspicious. The money in the writers' room kept them all there. They would not leave even if their bodies began to self-consume. Coral's lie would not be an escape, only a delay. They would all stay until they decayed.

The new Jay that Coral built on her phone had the potential to be anyone, and so she considered the men she wanted to know. She knew more men she did not like than those she wanted to call brother. There were tech bros and pseudo artists, all of whom acted like parasites on ideas from smarter people in presumed-weaker bodies. These were the men Coral worked with, an exercise much like goat yoga, where something quite nourishing is unnecessarily interrupted with an animal leaping onto your back. You are supposed to think it is cute but are decidedly in distress. They also poop periodically.

Coral could see the vastness of the city as she walked to the edge of the lot. When people thought much of themselves they were always situated on hills. Coral admired the view, the greenery swelling against the concrete structures, the movement of cars, and the ribbons of the roads knotting and unfurling.

In the Clinic for Dying While Willfully Participating in a Poorly Thought-Out Cultural Trend and Becoming a Martyr for Revolution, we help our little brother put on a tie, meaning we watch as our father aggressively demonstrates putting on a tie. The act is simple yet mysterious. Our father is not a skilled teacher and enters the task frustrated. We are certain we could do the task with ease, and then do so. We admire our throat in the mirror. We are young, almost a woman, and we look good. Our success is ignored by our father because the pointlessness of a girl tying a tie around her own neck is unamusing to him. We demonstrate our superiority to our brother in intellect and hand-eye coordination, and we are scorned with silence.

Jay's phone begins to ring and ring in Coral's pocket and with terrifying carelessness she almost answers on instinct. She sees the caller's face, Khadija as a thirteen-year-old, a very old picture from when she was overweight with bangs blowing back off her face like a crinkled curtain lifting to the sky. She is smiling hard. It is a terrible photo. In that brief space of forgetting who she was and the limitations of her own body, she nearly answered the phone and believed Jay's own voice would come out of her mouth, a deep bass in a permanent state of suspicion whenever he said the word *hello*. Then she remembered that Khadija's father, her brother, was dead. Coral smiled at Khadija's not-knowing and hummed before silencing the phone.

The Friday before Jay's death, he, Coral, and Khadija went to dinner at La Vaquita. They sat at one of the three booths they always sat in for a Friday dinner once a month or so. Khadija had been quiet most of the evening. She put her order in with the server at a volume so low he had to ask her twice what she was saying. Coral eventually ordered the chicken enchiladas with beans. When the server left, Coral spoke again.

Why are you like this?

Like what?

Pretending all the time. You're not sad or weak. You put on the baby voice and become this.

Coral gestured in Khadija's direction.

Ask for what you want.

I don't want anything.

Ask for what you want and you might get it or you might not. But it's faster than all of this.

Coral's first girlfriend, when she was twenty-six years old, lived in Ontario, California. She lived with her grandmother, who traveled so frequently the girlfriend practically lived alone. The girlfriend identified as lesbian, a pastry chef (aspiring), a graduate student (chemistry), biracial, and left-handed. After spending an afternoon with the lesbian, pastry chef (aspiring), graduate student (chemistry), biracial, left-handed girlfriend, Coral returned to her father's home in Compton to find him dead. His mouth hung open like sleep, palms supine to the ceiling, and Coral knew instantly the sliver of light that had closed on her.

Coral's father and mother died in separate years, not too close together and not too far apart, though their lives nearly never intersected. For some reason, throughout her life, Coral had expected her mother to be dead at any moment, as though death was the karmic result of selfishness and poor dietary choices.

In the Clinic for Dying While Willfully Participating in a Poorly Thought-Out Cultural Trend and Becoming a Martyr for Revolution, we have a girlfriend for the first time and refuse to love her. Because we refuse to love her, we do not have to tell anyone about her aside from a few close friends we've known since middle school, and even then we do not give this girlfriend a name, because that would make her more real and possibly worthy of deep and complex emotional attachment. When our niece asks us why we don't have a boyfriend, we say, *We are busy.* Our niece nods in confusion and tries to become busy as well, drawing in books and arranging stickers meticulously.

We have studied the correlation between grief and sex, how those in mourning are often extremely horny. We wonder if it is an assertion of life, a biological reflex, possibly related to repopulation. We doubt that very much.

It was once believed that couples who die shortly after each other must have been in love. We have conclusive evidence regarding that particular theory. Grief of any kind can be fatal; it consumes the consciousness and latches on to the senses that care for practical things like breathing, eating croissants, or anything at all.

In the Clinic for Dying While Willfully Participating in a Poorly Thought-Out Cultural Trend and Becoming a Martyr for Revolution, we ride in the passenger seats of cars. These cars are driven by people we love and are supposed to love but have a hard time finding the right frame of mind to do so. Our brother is in the driver's seat and our niece is in the back. She is fourteen and we have told her we are lesbian and she nods like an old woman. We tell her to tell her father. We are cowards, and we are cunning. The conversation is awkward and Jay turns up the music and pulls into Tam's Burgers and orders a #2 with a Coke. We know to wait. We do not look at our niece, her breathing and shifting and silence. The person on the other end of the drive-thru speaker mentions ketchup and our brother says, *What.* They repeat, *Ketchup.* Our brother again says, *What, what, what?*

Coral called her first girlfriend to say, *My father died.* The conversation is one Coral will never forget, one that made her deeply distrustful of people she met online, people that were left-handed and who believed in naturopathy. Coral's girlfriend said, *I'm so sorry to hear that* in a tone that suggested she was cuddling a puppy and had been satiated by a delicious meal under a cabana with the scent of pineapple and sunscreen. We are not sure where the girlfriend was exactly, but we are certain that she was happy wherever that might've been, somewhere far away.

Coral's mother died in December of 1994. The funeral was very different from any other Coral had been to or would go to again.

When mothers die, a peculiar thing happens. Whether the mother is good or bad or just fine does not matter. All mothers represent a vacancy; they are the ribbon around clouds, and the space between is filled with expectations, demands, reconciliations, disappointments, and fury.

The passenger seat of a car most often provided a soothing reprieve, when the car was in motion, that is. A space that could very well be a cage for some was often a realm of protection, submission, and trust. The passenger existed in a precarious state of both prisoner and companion.

Coral knew right away that her girlfriend was not alone on the other side of the phone. Grief is not binding, not a darkness; it can provide a special and sublime opening of the senses, the physical senses and the others for which we have no name. Coral could picture the familiar mouth, the richness of the voice, and all the familiar warmth of that person being tugged in another direction.

I'll call you later. I'm so sorry.

Coral could feel the smile on the other side of the phone.

Looking over Lankershim Boulevard from the studio lot, Coral texted Jay's phone from her phone.

Coral: I'm gay.

Jay: I know. U gay af.

Coral: When did you know?

Jay: Like when you were four.

Coral: Shut up.

Jay: It's cool. Men ain't shit.

Coral: Shut up.

Jay: No lie. Love you sis.

Coral: Love you too.

Having abandoned the effort to sleep ever again in life, Coral turned to Google searches of exes. She found the first girlfriend's Wikipedia page and decided to make some adjustments. She included horse veterinary studies on the résumé, which linked to a free porn page featuring hand-puppet fetishes. We think Coral loved the girlfriend more now.

Coral could not remember riding in a car with her mother. They lived in separate cities and traveled in separate vehicles, and still they knew each other in ways that would always matter before and after death.

After their father's death, Coral and Jay fought often. Coral had the credit card with the large available balance and so could make decisions about the funeral home, the obituary, and the burial site, which was the only thing prepaid. Coral was thankful. Jay was boastful.

In the Clinic for Dying While Willfully Participating in a Poorly Thought-Out Cultural Trend and Becoming a Martyr for Revolution, we bury our father. We believe the world has decided to actively work against every choice we make. Our brother, the last of our family, our hard heart, claims it was easy, claims that our father made it easy. *Already paid for*, he says to everyone that doesn't ask him. *Already paid for*, meaning the crypt. Much was not paid for: the casket, the funeral home, the flowers, the obituary, the unexpected hollowness in the bones and constriction of the upper respiratory system. When the limo company declines our card and threatens to cancel transportation, we throw our phone across the room.

In the Clinic for Dying While Willfully Participating in a Poorly Thought-Out Cultural Trend and Becoming a Martyr for Revolution, we ride in the passenger seat from Tam's Burgers to eat in the park with our brother and niece. We have just come out as gay minutes before. Our brother ordered the food, and it has been quiet for a long time. He says, *Do you want to see* X-Men *this weekend? Matinee?* We say, *Yeah.* In the passenger seat with the windows rolled down, we feel a light again where there wasn't one. Sometimes we call it home.

After a series of text messages to friends that end in variations of *fuck that bitch*, Coral stopped talking to the left-handed girlfriend. She did so via a method referred to as ghosting, meaning she simply stopped responding to any contact as though she'd died, meaning she weaponized silence in order to inflict the pain of loss upon someone who had inflicted a different variation of pain. Who died specifically is a curious matter. Perhaps the one that reaches out is treated like the dead, or maybe it is the one that is being contacted that must pretend to be gone from this world. Both scenarios work, though one is more satisfying than the other, depending on the circumstances.

In all these realities the correlation between grief and sex is constant. The body yearns for more than is possible.

Wildfire

BY CORAL E. BROWN

6. Red Autumn

Sex was certainly crucial for humanity, but so was murder. We estimate thirteen thousand methods of exterminating one another had been tried and tested up until the very end, but the method most dastardly and perhaps elegant and thorough took place at an event chronicled among the living that survived: Red Autumn. It had very much to do with the unnamable thing and humanity's desperate collective desire to dissolve it. Generational dysfunction

was a perpetual, cyclical state of being,
but when the penultimate generations es-
sentially made a heaping cesspool of the
planet, the generation to follow had no
mercy in exacting a most deadly revenge
for inheriting a scorched and polluted
earth with little knowledge about how to
correct it. There was a point when the
punishment tore at their bodies, disease
spread unchecked, poverty became equivalent to living, and everyone chose violence and received it in return. A kind
of exhaustion spread like a plague among
the people, one so vast and unyielding we
considered cataloging this period as the
great sleep, a fatigue so deep in the psyche that many died from inertia, from apathy, from ennui. Beautiful it was not, as
much as we can ascribe beauty to things
in motion, even if they are still as pho-
tographs. An object, a thought, must still
hum with a tendril of purpose, knowing,
or destiny to be beautiful, as we understand beauty. Red Autumn did not hum with
purpose, knowledge, or destiny. It was an
emptying of a Species, an upchuck of failure and loss. Only some of the oldest in
_____'s era remember the actual
days of Red Autumn, how dying seemed no
different from being born, where nihil-
ism required too much thought, too much
energy, too much hate to even manifest

among a Species so eternally and psycho-
logically weary of itself that it could
not muster enough disgust to even put its
own corpse in the ground. All lost touch
with the ordinary tribalism and competition for resources that gave people a
sense of themselves, to whom they belonged, whom they fought for, whom they
lived for, whom their deaths would please.
Death no longer pleased anyone, and all
any of those still living could do was
count the objects that did not survive
the sleep, the things they had no will to
produce, because they had no stomach for
pleasure or comfort or pain or anything.

The things lost but not forgotten were
varied and incredible: peanut butter, lard,
incense, grapeseed oil, mascara, char-
coal, cinnamon, pancakes, gauchos, rosary
beads, gooey duck meat, sand, jewel bee-
tles, frostbite, sincerity, sausages, pine
needles, devotion, whipped cream, tofu,
honey, tea, hilarity, poppy seeds, rice
pudding, silk, vanity, and all the rest.
Out of the great dying came the great
sleeping and then the great remembering,
all of which make up the total period of
Red Autumn, thirteen years. It took humanity thirteen years to decide to try
again. Hopeful, this sounds, and as far
as we can tell that hope might be inaccurate on the whole for what the pe-

riod really meant. Hope too vanished in phase one of Red Autumn, only to make a strange, mutated resurgence in the final hours. Those that lived and dared to remember all the things lost carried with them one thing so powerful they could not break the unnamable thing between themselves and the dead: resentment. Oh, how the children loathed their parents and their parents' parents and so on and so forth. This is, of course, in the wide-lens sense of things, because how can a child resent the ashes of an ancestor so far removed they have no body or face or voice? Without a voice to despair, humans struggle to maintain the punitive and cruel displeasure necessary for their own survival. They hated the very thing that linked them to generations that were so poorly organized that death and life were no longer distinguishable. The children committed the singular act of survival, which burst forth from life once again after it had shriveled to less than an atom. The children forgot their names. Humans love to name one another. There is little else more powerful than the declarative sentence, the order of words that makes a thing real or false, regardless of reality. The power to name is the power to judge, to gift, and to poison, to plant and to plunder. The names of all humanity

were recorded in a separate volume, their
villains and their deities, their grifters
and their hairdressers, legends and loi-
terers alike. All erased. No child would
ever bear the name of the dead again. Instead, the living turned to their catalogs
of lost things. The great remembering became their legacy. We wonder if it proved
effective, but one would need to agree on
a goal in order to judge the results. If
the goal was to prolong the life of the
Species, perhaps we can say yes. The Species was destined to reach an inevitable
conclusion, so we must agree on a measurement of time, time with value applied
to every minute of every year, with more
being greater than less, but we do not
do that, because some years are long and
uneventful while some minutes are thrilling and devastating. We value time as it
blooms but not for how long a clock de-
termines its being. To us it always exists, in the tomes where beginnings have
endings and each life shines like a mar-
ble, perfect and spherical, of infinite
existence.

Returning to death—as with all murders,
the killers required souvenirs—perhaps the
naming of newborns after extinct flora and
fauna gave the people a sense of creation.
That would hold true with many cannibal-
istic practices noted before Red Autumn.

Humans used to hunt their enemy tribes, then eat the flesh or drink the blood, and when that became too trying they would pretend to eat the flesh and drink the blood of their gods in places of worship. They often fed their dead to carrion birds, or exhumed corpses and danced with them. Ritual gave them life or reminded the living that they were not dead. In any case, during Red Autumn, many died, then remembered to live for a while longer, but death of the imagination was not as easily undone.

TUESDAY

IN THE Clinic for Weaponizing Fame in Order to Achieve Public Adoration and a Cover for Myriad Crimes, we attend a comic convention. We are a panelist at a comics festival in Los Angeles. We wait in a bleak space that is a series of dark curtains erected in a room with glass ceilings so high they feel like part of the natural sky.

The Los Angeles Convention Center, located on South Figueroa Street, housed many events of note over the century and a half or so of its existence, including wedding expos, auto shows, megachurch services of various denominations, the American Society of Human Genetics annual meeting, and Herbalife achievement awards ceremonies. The Los Angeles Convention Center would be destroyed to make room for low-income housing that would shortly become high-income housing due to land scarcity. The structure swelled in its pocket of the city, shaped like a colossal battery.

There used to be comic conventions held all over the globe to celebrate fandoms of various degrees of sincerity, the uninhibited joy of reveling in the worlds that began in one mind and were inherited by millions to occupy in various mediums. Mostly, they were crowded. They were crowded arenas of deranged, inebriated, sloppy, judgmental, devoted, delirious, exhausted fanatics of books, animations, film, TV, and games that crossed the planet. These fans argued. They swooned. They wore costumes. They wore black T-shirts. They walked and walked and walked like drone ants set on task by their queen, an unyielding endeavor with no end. The attendees of every comic con were promised a chance to glimpse a creator, a chance to interact with someone that provided reprieve to their lives, enrichment to their lives, meaning to their lives. They were often enraptured. They were often disappointed.

Wigs: Then came the wigs. Wigs have long been a source of power and prestige for the Species from eras that have little record of language other than the blood in the stone. Wigs were crowns and titles, provided authority, wherein the naked head of a man or a woman lacked substance. Wigs were formed from the hair of the poor and sat upon the heads of the wealthy.

At a comic convention, wigs were brightly colored, unnatural to human biology but near perfect in color matching to the invented characters of artificial worlds. Sure, there was a kind of fun to be had, but ultimately a singular driving force pressed the masses to the convention center doors: sex. Young women wore painstakingly crafted costumes of fictional damsels, princesses, warriors, and East Asian schoolgirls with hair any shade found in a rainbow. Men dressed up too, but not with the same level of public expectation and theater. Comic conventions served as thinly veiled group therapy for persons not yet accustomed to going to sex parties but who really would enjoy them.

Eventually every comic convention would be precursory to an orgy.

.   .   .

In the Clinic for Weaponizing Fame in Order to Achieve Public Adoration and a Cover for Myriad Crimes, we have fans. We are not really wealthy and we are not really famous, but there are some on earth who adore us. They've watched us be interviewed for podcasts and speak at conferences. They've watched videos of us sketching characters on a whim and others for production in a beloved series. They believe in the worlds we've created and want to thank us for that faith. Our fans are intellectuals and students and are often alarmed by other comic convention attendees' antics, such as vomiting from anxiety when in the presence of an actor that played an aquatic superhero. Our fans wear black and often have dreadlocks. Small quotes are tattooed on the sides of fingers. If people were dinosaurs, our fans would be tiny and nimble, and would know how to hide deep in trees, camouflaged and watching, curious and delighted by the carnivorous opera playing out before them.

Coral expected to meet several young women with aspirations toward writing and dreams of creating a cartoon that inspires another generation of young women to aspire to write and to create cartoons. Coral saw herself as a bead on a chain, sparkly but insignificant. She considered the chain without her bead, gently sewing itself together as if she had never been there, had never mattered one tiny, tiny bit. Should Coral continue in this vein, in some years she would be aged and less admirable but possibly more self-aware or possibly infinitely less aware of herself and the world and subject to all manner of ridicule and isolation and retinol serum routines.

The dark curtains that conceal the panelists/presenters/ spectrum of celebrities from the ordinary attendees are heavy and resistant to showing stains or wear. These curtains have endured many bodily secretions, the sweats and oils of anxious humans emptying out their desire to be seen, to be loved. Major celebrities cannot wait long behind the curtains for the rational fear that they will be smelled out by fans and loved in painful, irreparable ways. So they are ushered in quickly to their designated areas, then ushered out with similar speed and efficiency. They don't get as acclimated to the scent of the place, the salt and musk and carbon dioxide that fill the cavernous arena to the brim. Coral, however, was not a major celebrity but one safe behind the dark curtains for indefinite amounts of time. If her fans found her, they were more likely to offer her a beverage than throw themselves on her body, all risk of arrest be damned, for the chance to feel her skin against theirs and know forever that they have lived that moment just the once. Because Coral had no danger of that kind of love, she was left alone for a long while. A different kind of danger occurs in that box of time and separation. The danger of worry, insecurity, contemplation of worth, failure, insignificance, embarrassment at having tried to give a gift to someone, a thing brand-new so not yet assigned an assumed value, a thing that may be denied acceptance, denied the right to be at all. With those dangerous thoughts comes the worst of all sensations for someone like Coral, the emptying out of everything: loneliness.

It'll be just a few more moments. The books finally arrived.

A pleasant voice, feminine and kind, pierced the curtains. Coral nodded and offered thanks. The kindness of the voice could not shake the sudden wave of claustrophobia and hollowness in Coral, so she put a piece of sugarless gum into her mouth and opened an app on her phone. The reprieve of a digital space was less of a salve and more of a bad medicine.

Of all the apps Coral chose to open in order to dilute the time sloshing around her, heavy as quicksand, she chose a dating app. The online dating process during this era was one of utter and total misery and disillusionment, especially for those with strong communication skills. The less words one used, the more "successful" the experience, meaning the more connections made and the more real-world meetings scheduled. Coral had excellent language skills and also a knack for reading the natural sense of language possessed by others. She would avoid proper punctuation, grammar, or excessive syllables if the woman was attractive enough and used a lot of lowercase *i*s to refer to herself. The process was much like dipping one's head into a magmatic vein protruding from an active volcano. All humans would eventually try anything to feel more than nothing.

Coral peeked out of the curtains to scan the crowd and was overwhelmed by all the hair, the sea of black T-shirts, the crush of bodies moving along invisible guided pathways, a semblance of order where chaos loomed in agitation, waiting for the time to strike and send everyone into a panic.

The perplexing range of hair-care routines implemented by the Species was on full display at the convention: The I-don't-give-two-shits style dominated. The I-literally-woke-up-like-this coifs followed in numbers right before This-took-an-hour-but-you-would-think-I-barely-tried and a few of the I-paid-three-hundred-dollars-for-this-cut-and-color-and-it-was-fucking-worth-it looks dotted the remaining population.

In the Clinic for Weaponizing Fame in Order to Achieve Public Adoration and a Cover for Myriad Crimes, we tip excessively in places where we are recognized by strangers. This does not occur often. It happens at book signings in libraries, art institutions, and specialized conventions. We order coffee and tip 200 percent and think about phrases like *retirement plan* and *investment portfolio* and *diversified planning* as if they are prayers.

We sketch schematics on hair now, measure out the dimensions of prestige or poverty, adjust for the century and the ethnic sphere of influence. Our schematics resemble blueprints for cities and aqueducts. Hair was never accidental; it was a demonstrator of status and preparedness for every human interaction.

We wear the hair of mourning most often, cut short out of fatigue and in the haste to remove memory from the body and make room for life again. Cutting hair after a great loss soothed those who were left to breathe alone. Grief lived in hair, so the wise knew to take it off as soon as possible.

Jay's head was nearly smooth the last time Coral saw him alive, a week or so before the comic con. His eyes were tired, double bags filled with salt water and anxiety. Jay never wore glasses like Coral did; he also worked jobs that required few screens and even fewer words to read. He worked for the city and had a shirt with his name stitched onto the chest pocket and used heavy-duty gloves.

In the Clinic for Weaponizing Fame in Order to Achieve Public Adoration and a Cover for Myriad Crimes, we cook a Christmas ham. It is Compton, California, in 1994, and we are fifteen years old. Girls our age do not make ham as well as we do. Girls our age do not usually make ham at all. Vinyl records play the Jackson 5 because our father believes vinyl is the best sound. We believe him always. He is on the phone and is upset, so we check on our ham. It smells and sounds like heaven. Our brother runs in to look in the oven too, and we push him away. He tries to use his new teenage strength but is still too weak when we pull his rattail at the base of his scalp. There are pineapples and maraschino cherries on the meat that are beginning to blacken. Our father puts his head in one hand and listens to the phone with the other.

When Jay was fifteen he had a neighbor braid his hair, loose braids that hung down from the top of his head and settled just above his ears. Coral laughed and laughed and laughed and laughed and laughed and never knew why that moment, over all the years and conversations they would later have, would never be forgiven.

In the Clinic for Weaponizing Fame in Order to Achieve Public Adoration and a Cover for Myriad Crimes, we eavesdrop on a conversation with bad news. Our mother was in the hospital. We had not seen her in some years. When our father hangs up the phone, he asks us how much longer till the ham is ready. We say, *Now*. The ham we made is our aunt's recipe and it is the second time we have made it alone. The Aunts screamed in delight the first time we made Christmas dinner without help from an adult. That night, we cut our brother's rattail off while he sleeps.

As far as fan wigs were concerned, no one color dominated, but some colors possessed more connotative weight than others. The blond ponytail wig, for example, served as an iconic nod to beloved feminist characters from Japanese animation that crossed national and gender boundaries.

The ubiquitous schoolgirl outfits were undoubtedly salacious and subject to pervy gazes and manipulations, but were still the uniform of power in training. The lessons would be painful and to some traumatizing, but if learned, there could be currency extracted from the eyes that leered at the pleated skirts and bows tied across the chests.

In contrast to the soft cotton and nylon fabric of school uniforms were the warriors, the hard metals and plastics that composed the armor of these vixens and heroines, skillfully designed to accentuate cleavage and thighs. This armor was crowned in silver wigs or dark braids with pink or red accents.

Coral's fans wore business suits, double-breasted, with skirts and round mirrored sunglasses, and carried artificial 9-millimeter handguns tucked under their arms, or at least they did until security banned weapon facsimiles from the conventions. Their wigs were black locs with white accents. They looked like certified public accountant rock stars.

The curtains parted again in a dramatic swish of air. Coral's eyes watered. A few dozen people waited in line for a signed copy of her graphic novel. Someone said *Finally* in exasperation. Coral stood and remembered the masks and the costumes everyone wore and felt comforted knowing none of this was real.

As an infant, Coral was exceptionally bald, with patchy smooth skin across the back and sides of her heavy head. In her baby photos she was as cute as any baby, maybe even cuter than most babies, due to the haphazard bows that gripped fine and wistful snatches of hair from the pools on her slick scalp.

Then came the pigtails and barrettes. Yellow hearts and purple birds were Coral's favorite. They clicked like dull wind chimes whenever she moved her head. There were still bald spots, but they were fewer, and Coral's words grew more abundant. She spoke like an adult. That was second grade.

In the Clinic for Weaponizing Fame in Order to Achieve Public Adoration and a Cover for Myriad Crimes, we are bullied as a child for having our father style our hair poorly every day. We have tightly curled hair like most other children in our neighborhood, but where their hair is thick and luminescent, ours is thin and dry. We identify the weaknesses of our bullies: their poverty and slow speech. We speak to our bullies in sentences that do not break, faster than they can understand. We attack their parents' finances. We attack their shoelaces. We attack the spaces between their teeth. Our audience is enthralled and afraid. We make them laugh and we make others quiet.

Later came the perms. Coral's father gave up on pretending to be able to do everything a mother can and things some mothers can't. He took Coral to a professional hairdresser and paid more money than he would for a week of groceries.

Coral's hair fell out in chunks and only her father cried. Coral did not cry or grimace. She'd come to expect nothing other than losing a little more of something every day than she had the day before. Ownership always felt like pretend.

While standing in the small partitioned area waiting to meet the crowd, Coral added two photos to her dating profile. The pictures were waiting to be approved while she examined the worthiness of inclusion, one photo with long hair and another with short; one photo with a closed mouth and an expression of longing, the other jubilant, teeth glistening in the sun.

In her pocket she felt the familiar buzz of Jay's phone. She welcomed the sensation and the feeling of continuity that came with it. Someone somewhere cared for him, wanted to seek his counsel and companionship. She appreciated that knowledge, along with some other feeling we've called jealousy before but are no longer so certain.

Coral was escorted by the elbow to a plastic chair in front of a foldout table covered with a black cloth and stacked with her books. In the time between walking and finally sitting, Coral saw a message from Summer to Jay that urgently wanted to confirm their Thursday meeting.

There was a way to delay that encounter and a very good reason not to agree at all. Coral needed time to consider the response and to make the buzzing cease for a few moments.

Jay: Sorry had some paperwork for K to do.

The buzzing ceased. Coral could read Summer well enough to know that mentioning Khadija would be serious enough to warrant silence and uncertainty.

Outside the partitioned area the air circulated more freely, cooler but no less stale, with drifts of sunbeams piercing the crowd and their shadows. Coral's small group stood in a ribboned line carved with nylon belts on metal poles. She felt a familiar kind of happiness or a mimicking sensation, like that produced by narcotics.

Coral became a wizard now that she'd left the curtains, and to those that came to see her she possessed knowledge and an ability they envied and adored. Coral wore loose pleated trousers with a brown leather belt and a cardigan like a grandfather's, along with long gold chains, as a pimp might. She was striking.

Then Coral noticed the face of the staff member that had spoken to her and kept her isolated for so many minutes. It was the face of a human who could not care less about the spectacle before them. Coral almost laughed at the sincere apathy in the staff member's straight lips. They had long green nails, poorly managed acne and scarring, and a mustache like a 1970s detective.

The staffer checked their watch and not a cell phone for the time. Coral wondered where they had to be other than here, other than this place, where Coral was loved in a way she felt nowhere else on earth. Then she wondered how sincere this love was, how close to a betrayal it might be if she said the wrong thing or made the wrong joke.

Breathing became a little more challenging under the weight of a sudden awareness of her own fragility as a human being.

Then the signings began, easy and efficiently. Coral signed thirty-two books, smiled, posed for photos, received some fan sketches, and took photos to post and tag with the fan's handles. She reveled in the separation of this time from other times. Then came the lull. The line had emptied and the floor was visible with dropped flyers and programs.

With some ridiculous instinct toward hope, Coral looked up at the staffer, expecting an exchange of words, another opportunity for brief human connection, but the staffer had retreated into a tablet, so Coral immediately turned to her own technology for everything she'd missed up till that moment.

The dating app opened first and Coral weighed her options. To make her profile available in that environment with the proximity settings as they were was like jumping into a swamp infested with crocodiles. Hungry lesbian nerds swam in the waters of a comic con ready to snap any new profile into a death spiral.

There were worse things in this life than public embarrassment and digital shame. Coral hit ACTIVATE on her profile in a fleeting act of ambivalence. The empty line might've given her the impression that this place was somewhere else, vacant of queers thirsty for bodily contact, a place like Merced.

A few more people entered the area leading to Coral's

booth. The staffer had already strategically altered the nylon belts to hasten the journey from entry to the table. Simultaneously the dings began on Coral's phone, alerts from the app, likes, messages. This was not uncommon. New profiles always attracted the most attention.

As a young, inexperienced lesbian in a foreign city, Coral began her online dating journey with a desktop computer before there were handheld smartphones and vast digital access to romantic encounters. The city was Phoenix, and like many cities with interesting food, a smallish population, and environmentally devasting conditions, it was generally low on queers.

In the Clinic for Weaponizing Fame in Order to Achieve Public Adoration and a Cover for Myriad Crimes, we are on a bad date. Our date is a liar. She has admitted to it twice, once about her real name and once about her job. We do not know who she is or how to address her and never will. She arranges a meeting at a coffee shop that serves acai bowls, which she claims are delicious, but does not order anything to eat or drink. She speaks to the workers with a familiarity that leaves us perplexed. She sits across from us and talks about music-related things, ambitions, achievements. We do not understand. We are never asked questions. We listen. We nod. We open our mouths in the way one does when they are about to speak and say nothing. We eat blueberries and almond slivers and wish to evaporate.

The dings persist as the convention fans approach.

· · ·

In the Clinic for Weaponizing Fame in Order to Achieve Public Adoration and a Cover for Myriad Crimes, we are on a very bad date. Our date is beautiful and smiles often. We tell her we graduated from high school younger than most and earned scholarships to graduate school. We tell her we've bought houses and traveled internationally. She is smiling and miserable, and we are blind to it all.

Coral's and Jay's phones began to ding in harmony, a mild, anxiety-inducing symphony of staccato notes. Coral put them both face down on the black tablecloth. She began to sweat and felt her heart accelerate, as was common in a panic attack. This was uncommon for Coral, so she believed she was having a heart attack.

Are you okay? the previously apathetic staffer asked.

I'm dying, Coral replied.

The staffer lifted Coral by the elbow with ease, gathered her things from the table and floor, then ushered her back behind the curtain, where they did not stop but continued to walk through a series of other curtains until they arrived at a black unmarked door. The staffer opened the door and then they were in a restroom.

Take a minute. Breathe. I'll be just outside.

Coral was alone.

In the Clinic for Weaponizing Fame in Order to Achieve Public Adoration and a Cover for Myriad Crimes, we are in elementary school on the toilet, constipated. The stalls have no doors. We are an excellent student and have unlimited hall-pass privileges. Whenever we finish our assignments early we ask to go to the bathroom, even when we don't need to. That day, however, we ate fourteen ounces of sharp cheddar cheese in one sitting. We will never do this again. We believe we are going to die.

When Coral exited the bathroom, she didn't look at her own reflection, just at the floor and the stall doors and the handles. The staffer stood outside, unchanged, an expression of genuine concern and understanding still on their face. Coral did something close to a smile but really just showed her teeth like a horse.

Can I tip you? she asked.

The staffer snorted.

No.

Can I buy you a margarita then?

In the hour between lunch and dinner, when bars and restaurants are not quite full and not quite empty, Coral found a seat at a counter alone. No one was coming to see her, no one knew where she was. She sketched a full moon on a napkin and held it up to the fluorescent lights above. The bartender nearby glanced at her, then away.

You should do napkin art, Coral said. *Hang it up.*

What? he said, drawing a glass of beer.

Napkin art, on the mirror or wall.

What?

Napkin art?

What?

Art?

What?

While retreating into her email inbox to swim in the unsolicited ads for leather booties, arts and crafts, and subscription reminders for streaming service renewals, Coral was startled by an enthusiastic fan. The fan said, *Excuse me*, and was so close to Coral's ear that she felt a small fleck of saliva, cold and dense.

She'd seen many faces and almost faces at the convention, the kind that don't exactly blur but fold in and out of one another like cabinets opening and closing except with noses and upper lips. Coral was sure she'd seen that upper lip before, feminine and streaked with hairs lightly bleached. There was nowhere to escape to while sitting heavily on the barstool and pinned in by the young woman. After resolving to be held captive by the stranger for an indeterminate amount of time, Coral realized there was no harm to be had.

I missed the signing. They took you away in a hurry a few minutes before the end.

I'm so sorry.

Just as Coral spoke, the bartender turned on a blender to make three piña coladas for a handful of new drinkers. The bartender was in his late fifties and looked as though young people caused him indigestion.

Coral saw the copy of her comic stuck out in front of her with a pen.

What's your name?

Marissa.

Coral drew a picture of a revolver and signed her name on the handle and wrote, *Sorry I missed you the first time, Marissa*, in letters that looked like smoke emerging from the barrel.

OMG thank you!

Coral smiled almost and nodded, alone again once Marissa left. The bartender in his black shirt and red tie was watching her. He seemed to have noticed Coral for the first time since she'd sat down half an hour prior.

An opportunity to speak came and evaporated just as quickly before the bartender began loading dirty glasses into a crate and took them through a door and out of sight.

The range of hairstyles Coral had selected earlier in the day for her dating profile nagged at her psyche. Once she'd opened the app again to inspect her photos, she felt dismayed and then curious. She knew those women well, those slightly younger versions of herself, their angst and insecurities about the missing tooth that shows if she laughs too hard, the birthmarks, the frequent loss of interest in a conversation that is often interpreted as a loss of interest in the person she's conversing with.

Coral felt a wave of despair and helplessness and wanted to cast a line for salvation in any way possible, and the only means of connection available was the message button on the app. She had two favorites to choose from. One was Shillana, black-haired and blue-eyed like Superman but with big boobs and a motorcycle. Her profile had grammatically sound sentences strung together with wit and ferocity. The other was Sita, a tattooed hiker with two sentence fragments in the profile that could only be interpreted as sociopathic narcissism. Coral wanted to be disposable. She did not want to be kept. She messaged Sita.

Somewhere in the marvelous space of who-gives-a-fuck, Coral proceeded to message more women with less regard for personality or profile picture. She took out Jay's phone and texted Summer again. She was the one Coral really wanted now. She was the one that did not respond right away, and like all who make themselves less available, that made her exponentially more desirable.

For unbearable seconds or minutes or less than seconds, Coral was perplexed and self-conscious as she considered Jay's voice. Did she sound too needy? Did Jay use participles and adverbs? She could not remember and held her own throat. She scratched at her neck as one might at an allergic reaction. She needed something like air but better.

Summer: I'm busy.

Coral was relieved. Her breath came and she realized she did not even know the shape of Summer's nose or her height and was panicked over an imagined woman that did not belong to her at all. Coral laughed. It was all a show, the theater of the heterosexuals. Woman feigns paying attention to another life. Man feels abandoned and desperate. Woman dangles her attention at the man. Man lunges. Coral was impressed with the simple tactic Summer deployed and wanted to congratulate her on such cunning.

Then Coral needed to vomit. She ran to the nearest restroom, hand pressed over her mouth while every stranger dodged out of her way, recognizing the terrifying urgency to move. Summer and Coral would never be friends, and the impossibility of their knowing each other and all the reasons why seized Coral like a flu. She remained for many minutes emptying herself as the automatic seat cover rotated periodically.

Instead of going home and napping off the emotional and physical exertion of interacting with dozens of people, smiling over trauma, and throwing up profusely from the effort of it all, Coral went back to the bar and reclaimed her vinyl stool and sea-salt-dusted counter. At that moment when she placed herself among people and most needed to be alone, Marissa returned.

The incidental crying Coral did in the bathroom had washed her eyes some, and all the world, especially Marissa, became more vivid—the cat eyeliner forming a smudged point into burgeoning crow's-feet, the wateriness of her eyes, which made Coral squint. She almost said, *What happened to you?* The change in Marissa was as pronounced as the change in Coral.

Being alone had been the enemy earlier, but now Coral missed it. She missed the cold tile floor under her knees and the whir of the air filters overhead in the restroom. The flow of cold water had soothed her. Now she was back in the hot, stale air of the bar, which began to feel more like a greenhouse as the day progressed.

Marissa began to stammer and Coral had a hard time understanding a whole sentence in between the *um*s and *like*s and tics, but she did notice the pen Marissa held, the same pen Coral had signed her book with. Marissa clicked it repeatedly from nerves, the ballpoint emerging and retreating with a loud snap.

Isn't her death playing into the kill-your-gays trope when they were like destined to be lovers and could've had like everything 'cause it's um hard for us like you know in the you know like this, and Marissa gestured to the universe.

Coral didn't move her eyes from that pen as Marissa's sweaty grip around it tightened like a fist, the end emerging to form a pointed hammer with Marissa's arm. Fights were common at comic cons. Celebrities were sometimes verbally assaulted, or actually assaulted. Coral did not expect that for herself, being so low on the tier of valuable people. One must be very loved to be hated.

What do you have to say? Marissa asked, the tip of her pen-hammer on the counter.

Everyone has an opinion, Coral answered, not knowing what was happening or what she was accused of. Marissa apologized and left.

In her car, Coral turned the AC on high and leaned into the vents.

Summer: do you want to try slots or tables?

Jay: You know I hate slot machines!

Summer: Just confirming :)

Jay: First hand is on me then.

Coral didn't wait long for Summer's response to that: an enthusiastic *OK!* and a smiley face. Summer sounded like a lot of fun.

In the Clinic for Weaponizing Fame in Order to Achieve Public Adoration and a Cover for Myriad Crimes, we are on a date with a woman who loves to watch short videos on her phone of people hurting themselves, getting into fights with fast-food workers, cats engaging in theatrical antics at two a.m., politicians making horrific and inappropriate statements to large audiences, and celebrities being arrested. We are not sure if this is a bad date or a good date but feel as though we are supposed to be impressed, that our date wants to impress us with the images that make her laugh and gasp. We feel as though years are shedding off our life like dander as the seconds pass.

·   ·   ·

While in her car, having cooled down from the events of the day, Coral began to search for more information on Summer. She felt a deep sense of satisfaction at being able to navigate gambling preferences with no information at all, but felt that much of the exchange rested on luck. She wanted to be more prepared, yes, for an impossible encounter or at least for another round of texts. In the online search, Coral instead discovered classmates of Jay's, mostly deceased. They were Black men nearing middle age in obituaries, next to classic cars, bronze and chrome, or at family barbecues, some slightly intoxicated and all happy. These were their final photos to the world.

In the Clinic for Weaponizing Fame in Order to Achieve Public Adoration and a Cover for Myriad Crimes, we wear a white wig and witch's hat with our mother. It is the only Halloween we share with the woman as far as we can remember. We are in a photo, and instead of a memory we have a memory of looking at the photo. Our mother is holding brown liquor over ice in one hand and us by the other. She looks at our face as we look at the camera. Everyone is smiling and everyone is surprised.

In the Clinic for Weaponizing Fame in Order to Achieve Public Adoration and a Cover for Myriad Crimes, we wear a mask. The mask is rubber and hot and the shape of a burned pedophile. We wear a striped shirt and gloves with artificial knives where there should be fingers. As a teenager we feel terrifying. Our younger brother wears a hockey mask from a different generation and carries a chain saw without a chain. The chain saw is not a toy; it growls when pulled to start and we do not like it but pretend to have no fear. We patrol the neighborhood in our masks and in our thunder for the night. We are alive.

In the Clinic for Weaponizing Fame in Order to Achieve Public Adoration and a Cover for Myriad Crimes, we take our six-year-old niece trick-or-treating at the mall. She is excited, but we hurry from store to store quickly because we are supposed to meet our age-appropriate friends later. Our niece is a princess in a black wig and yellow nylon dress. She cried because she wanted the blond wig, though we said no because it looked ridiculous. The preparation for the evening took many hours longer than the trick-or-treating. We feel we have gone above and beyond what was expected. In the end satisfaction eluded us all.

Anemone Gets a Dick (Part I)
Wildfire fanfic by queerbanana

Anemone served as _____'s physician.

If there is anything we know for sure about the total *Homo sapiens* when in full bloom and outside of the fearsome grip of nature but nestled safely within their own universe, one of independent creation and self-design, it is that they revel in routine. It is ceremonious. It is obsessive. It is disturbing only because they did not recognize it yet and fell into rigid patterns of thought and behavior so dutifully. When not living as a debt collector, _____ exercised the maniacal habit of routine. She lived as aunt, as head of household, as sister, watching her family roam around the house like bad drones in a poorly managed insect colony with too few inhabitants and a vague system of hierarchy. Everything was clean. Doors in the home were opened, then they were shut. _____ stood on one side of a door and someone else on another. She dressed. Then she worked. She made no contact with any human being other than Anemone and only if _____ was scheduled for one of two annual checkups or was *magnificently ill*, as Anemone would say.

Our existence depends on analysis, pattern recognition, so to observe such a careless inability to self-reflect is alarming. Still, here we are with _____ and studying an era so prideful about its disconnect from observable destructive behaviors, committing entirely to habits of malfeasance as if they were coffee in the morning. Citizens of the Nation lived out their duplicitous lives with zeal and meticulous execution. Because of this, accidental overlap in their personas was rightly shunned. Of all the failures to endure, exposing one's other life was deemed worst of all. Citizens and noncitizen residents might operate as tour guides and hackers, debt agents and nannies, sex workers of various specialties and sous chefs. It was woefully common and also expected. The faces met, the debts accrued, the victories achieved, and the defeats suffered were not to be felt or known by the other side. The lives were coins, surfaces that would be joined but never seen.

On occasion, however, the coins split and two lives had to confront each other. Sometimes the strongest life survived but too often the shame of it all overwhelmed the person at the crest and little could be done other than Mercy.

_____ had the tremor of attraction ripple so deep that she caressed the seam of her two halves. _____ possessed unfettered access to the surveillance systems of the Corporation, and with a few data-entry points she could trace Anemone's movements and whereabouts anytime of the day. That would be a violation of written and unwritten protocol, to track the location of someone not under debt collections' interest. She did it anyway. In her office, with the afternoon sunlight behind her pressing in through the glass with the heat of an anxious crowd, _____ accessed the cameras the moment Anemone and _____ parted ways in front of the restaurant Noodles!!! We considered a timeline in which to anticipate these kinds of stalking events. A week, a day, an hour, a month—it is never easy to speculate about how long this thing will nag at the body and the consciousness before a person will act. For _____, it was two years. She wore designated attire number four, a double-breasted suit in lavender plaid

with cream buttons. _____ watched
the other half of her coin, Anemone, in
her dark, impenetrable gear, turn into
the twilight and then fritz into oblivion.
Then she walked a bit on-screen, then lingered and turned around. _____'s
pupils dilated and her heartbeat accelerated with the fantasy that maybe Anemone
wanted to see her too for as long as possible. For several minutes she vanished,
became invisible to all the eyes in all
their sockets, which any agent of the Nation could do from time to time during
the day without becoming suspicious. Then
Anemone actually arrived.

"_____, dearest of my dears,
tell me of the world!"

Anemone hurried inside the office,
closed the door, and immediately blocked
the monitor with her whole self. We suspect _____'s heartbeat accelera-
tion in that moment to be from fear of
discovery of her improper research, and
with the intelligence of Anemone as such
a threat and delight, _____ had
every justifiable reason to perspire with
dread at the collision of her selves.

"The world is much the same today,"
_____ said, "as the day before."

"And all our yesterdays have lighted
fools. You look terrifically austere this
afternoon."

Anemone fingered _____'s lapel.

"Your praise is always a joy."

"How about a snack instead. I have something special to show you. Tonight. You have made changes to your home in the last year or two. I want to see."

"Anemone . . ."

"Your brother and niece are off at that horrendously violent youth sporting event."

"It is a basketball game, and that is tonight. You are right."

Anemone leaned in as if to whisper a secret, salacious and urgent.

"Atrocious things," she whispered. "Sports."

_____ laughed. Anemone stood. She smiled. She took a deep breath and looked at the warmth of the day behind _____, her smile lilting just a bit, then back again like a pothos's dry roots watered. Anemone had full access to _____'s biological records and composed a formula that she and she alone would find most agreeable.

"Tonight," Anemone said loudly with arms stretched to the ceiling, then left before _____ could respond.

In the once-again-silent office, _____ turned off her monitor and faced the wall of glass behind her. Grids and blocks of composite stones, sky sliced by buildings. To know exactly what she was thinking would elevate the quality of our data records immensely, but we can of course only speculate that her thoughts were either about the hour, synthetic tuna sandwiches, the moment she witnessed her parents dying in the wake of Red Autumn, or what elaborate sexual activity Anemone had planned for the evening. We do not know for sure.

Based on all prior evidence, we can with near certainty say that _____ would not have guessed that Anemone, her longtime colleague and paramour and FWB extraordinaire, would arrive at her doorstep wearing a jacket fit for a seventeenth-century pirate and a miniskirt designed for a twentieth-century cheerleader except for the faux leather trim with a newly genetically augmented cellular constructed penis erect and hidden inside a buttercream cake.

http://fanfictions.net/Wildfire/mature/serial-relationship-coral-anemone-queerbanana-3106355076

Anemone Gets a Dick (Part II)
Wildfire fanfic by queerbanana

Returning to the primary narrative of _____ in somewhat chronological order is the esteemed scientist and health-

care provider Anemone, with her newly purchased biosynthetic penis pushed into a
cake for the aesthetic thrill of the gesture (we assume). Anemone, the scientist,
the vixen, the BBW, thicc, voluptuous sack
of peaches, and all the declarations of
desirability bestowed upon women of uncon-
ventional size, lust, and envy. Her form
diverted from the usual lithe athleticism
of the Nation, fashionable and state man-
dated. We gather that her ability to escape
scrutiny for her extraordinary physical
dimensions was due to the indispensable
talent of her mind, friends in high places,
or general ease with which she manipu-
lated data records to her personal agen-
das. In any case, she fucked aplenty, and
her suitors of varied genders came again
and again, perhaps for the thrill of creative coitus because predicting the sexual theater of Anemone proved challenging
to our best statisticians, another testament to her exceptional genius. The era of
_____, one of limitless technologi-
cal reach, rewarded minds such as Anemone's,
and in this moment a penile unit—fully
functional, responsive, and composed of
her very own DNA—was the prize.

"How much are you paying for this?"
_____ asked, on her knees in the
foyer, inspecting Anemone's genitals, now
free from the cake.

"Let's discuss a little later maybe."

There are universal notes in the human languages for things such as moonlight or pain. These sounds manifest in raised pitches, light squeaks, no matter the syntax of a sentence. They are there in every recorded song, diatribe, rant on a subway, solicitation at a quiet bar in the thick of the night. In the *maybe* rang that note of delight and pain, the formula for lust, the mating call of every lover in the mood to do the thing. Oh, the glory of fucking! The electrical energy produced can light up a city literally and metaphorically.

While Anemone lay in a state of delirious ecstasy beneath a steady lifting and sliding, _____ pulling against Anemone's brand-spanking-new hyper-grown dick (purchased through a reasonable payment plan) with her vagina, firm as a potato sleeved in silk, we considered the timeline of such a possibility.

Phalluses have been worshipped independently of men from the beginning of human record. Contrary to some of their own historical documents, the first image drawn on a cave wall was not of an animal used for food or companionship. It was of a penis, a thing of fascination and obsession for the brief span of human existence. This is not to be confused with

the gender identity wars, which sparked
a revolutionary renaissance of public acceptance of the spectrum of gender and
sexuality, one so brilliant and so free of
shame and so long desired that it survived
Red Autumn, along with industrial capitalism and nihilistic tribalism. Anemone's
ability to afford a penis was unique to the
Nation and to citizens with the financial
freedom to invest in such a luxury item.
The penis, the dick, the schlong, managed
to maintain its iconic status as an emblem
of immovable force, strength without the
burden of consciousness, pleasure without
the burden of foresight. It is no wonder
that the Nation would make them available
to its wealthiest citizens as a reminder
of all the wonders and reveries of life
that exist because of the Corporation, how
the very bodies they live in can be shaped
and constituted to match all the ideals,
abstract and concrete, that make up the
corporate culture. Indulgence of every
kind without consequence (as long as one
could afford it) became policy, law, a
Tuesday evening. Certainly, vaginas were
very popular too. After the gender wars,
egregiously large genitalia went out of
style for obvious reasons. A thing needs
beauty as well as practicability, leaving
some life force for the heart.

Anemone screamed her climax with the power of an opera diva, her left nipple firmly secured between _____'s teeth. Both partners satisfied enough for the moment, _____ scooped a chunk of cake from the platter on the nightstand and ate it.

"Are you not sharing?" Anemone asked.

_____ went into the kitchen for two plates, a knife, and two forks. She prepared cake for the both of them, and they ate silently, naked, for three minutes and six seconds.

"You seem to be living elsewhere," Anemone finally said.

There are many notes, musical without question, within the human vocal range. They are never taught. They are innate, a song written perhaps by the unnamable thing. Anemone sang the phrase of knowing concern, where one sighs all the answers but speaks words of curiosity to draw confirmation from an audience. They are songs of investigators, jilted lovers, or intuitive friends. They are songs not easily recognizable as what they are to the audience that hears them, based on our assessments up to this point.

"The resident that poisoned you has been expunged," Anemone continued. "I inquired after submitting my report."

"You are always diligent," _____

said, and smiled. "How is Zenith taking your new addition?"

"He takes it very well, I'm sure."

_____ nearly laughed, a smile for sure, a breathy exhalation with contracted facial muscles, but a full laugh we cannot confirm.

"I'm happy for you both."

_____ was not happy and it was obvious. Zenith, the husband, the barrier to eternal love and indulgence, was unfortunately a good guy.

"Is it the thing with Bees?"

"Is what the thing with Bees?"

"She's rejecting her citizenship birthright. The young are inclined to do that this season. It will not last. Vanity will trump their principles in the end."

"Is that what citizenship is? Vanity?" asked _____.

"Life is beautiful. Beauty is expensive. Call it vanity. Call it survival. They all want it eventually."

"Is that a historical truth?"

Anemone laughed and licked frosting from her fork.

"Hardly!"

Comments

Wyldfyre101: Got serious at the end but loved the silk and the potato! Hot.

Lemme_fly: _____ always killing the mood with her moral compass omg.

User3259798: Can't wait for the next installment. Love your work!

Skyrimjob99: Ughhhhhhhh now I have to wait for them to fall asleep and wake up to get going again. I'm patient though thank you for your awesome writing. It sounds just like C.E.B.

User4839282: Reply: I wouldn't say just like C.E.B. there are some nuances to the original that can't be imitated so easily but a fair attempt for sure.

Skyrimjob99: Reply: Dang. I agree though. It's close.

WEDNESDAY

CORAL'S MOTHER HAD many sisters who composed what Coral referred to as the Aunts, not just for the accuracy of the designation but for the unit they represented. The Aunts were a council of sorts, a kind of republic that conferred among one another and plotted against one another, formed factions and insurgencies, yet theoretically acted toward the same goal, which was judging Coral's behavior.

In the Clinic for Excavating Repressed Memories in Search of Solutions to Current Crises, we are at a family reunion in Demopolis, Alabama. We are eleven years old and wear overly large shorts with vertical green and gold stripes with coveted black Doc Martens that are a half size too small. Our younger cousin pulls our hair and we scream and fight him. He runs and the Aunts look at us as if we are alien, feral, and should feel ashamed. We outgrow our boots entirely in two months.

Coral was entering Jay's apartment when a representative of the Aunts called her. Coral banged her knee on the TV stand, which was too close to the door, because the apartment was too small to have a TV stand at all or much of anything beyond a chair, a table, and a bed. The sound of something breaking cut the quiet and Coral was unsure if it was her body or the furniture. In the requisite hesitation about not answering the phone when one has no energy left for the human world, Coral paused but yielded.

Hello.

Everything is fine, Coral chanted in between stories of her new contract and adventures at the comic con. The representative of the Aunts was pleased and Coral noted that the age in her voice was more pronounced than before. Coral wondered if anything was wrong.

Everything is fine, said the representative of the Aunts, who then asked, *Are you sure everything is okay?*

Everything is fine, Coral replied, and in between discussions of gardens and plagues they repeated, *Everything is fine. Everything is fine. Everything is fine. Everything is fine.*

In the Clinic for Excavating Repressed Memories in Search of Solutions to Current Crises, we are playing dominoes. Cicadas pulse and harmonize like electricity in the humid air. We sit at a picnic table in a park. We are wearing a yellow T-shirt with BROWN FAMILY REUNION on the front in expectantly brown letters. It is an ugly shirt. Here we learn to cheat intoxicated men out of their money. The adults are drunk and loose with cash and we sit like a man and talk like a man with a girl's vaguely pretty head and say *Pay me* to an uncle with such authority and humor that they all laugh like it is the first joke they've ever heard.

The TV stand in Jay's apartment is made of composite wood, a sign of a dark age. During this period, the Species mixed chemicals with artificial fibers to make an inexpensive product that looked like a natural substance and was ultimately devastating to the environment. The corner of the TV stand broke off and seemed to Coral like a thing that had broken off many times. She attempted to fix it, hunting for glue in Jay's dark apartment. She found the ubiquitous drawer of many things: batteries, scissors, duct tape, dried markers, and Sharpies, keys to mysterious locks, magnets, screws, pliers, ancient raisins, crumbs, business cards for electricians and an eyebrow threader, for some strange reason.

In the Clinic for Excavating Repressed Memories in Search of Solutions to Current Crises, we are aunts with gardens. Our gardens are beautiful, with sunflowers, succulents, rhododendrons, asparagus ferns. We have sensible pots neatly arranged. The ground is always wet and sparkles. We tell our niece that God lives in nature and helping things to grow is a special kind of living.

In a warm ember of imaginative thought, Coral told the Aunts' representative that Jay got a promotion.

That's wonderful! she squealed.

It'll be more of a desk job. He'll get to relax some, although he's always relaxing at work, in my opinion.

God is good.

Mmm-hmm.

Coral smiled and could feel the light from the Aunts, a sincere kind of joy, a connection to their sister through her. It seemed as real as the rough carpet scratching her knees as she knelt in front of the TV.

In the Clinic for Excavating Repressed Memories in Search of Solutions to Current Crises, we learn to play blackjack in Las Vegas. We are supposed to be in the dance club with our friends, but we are a closeted lesbian and tired of being groped by drunk men wearing Dior cologne. We play at a table with an old couple from Minnesota. They are patient and encouraging when we make a mistake and cheer when we win. We lose six hundred dollars, and it is the most we've ever risked and we are happy.

The glue failed to secure the corner of the TV stand, so Coral tried the duct tape. The result was hideous and made her angry.

In the Clinic for Excavating Repressed Memories in Search of Solutions to Current Crises, we are bingo-loving aunties. We've gone to casinos religiously for decades and have graduated to the final level of the culture: Sunday bingo regular status. There we clap in disgust and feign support when someone else yells bingo. Losing is a ritual.

We're going to celebrate his promotion later this week. I think his new girlfriend will be there too.

Ohhh, he's seeing someone now too. That's nice. What's his daughter's name again?

Khadija.

That's right. These names these days.

Coral felt insulted. She remembered the Aunts were not always kind, whether they meant to be or not. She remembered that they were full of judgment and self-righteousness and believed the world should be one way. They have never spoken of her sexuality and talked mostly of things to celebrate, and then Coral remembered the word *suffocation*.

I suspect there will be an announcement, Coral said.

What kind of announcement?

Marriage. Jay plans to propose.

That's wonderful, just wonderful. Is she a—well, nice woman?

A nurse, RN.

Oh wow.

She has a daughter too. Khadija likes her. I have to go check on my dinner cooking. It was nice catching up!

The representative of the Aunts said goodbye and Coral smiled into the dead phone. After some adrenaline-fueled effort, Coral managed to drag the broken TV stand down the iron stairs with a heavy clatter and hoisted it into the dumpster in the alley.

In the Clinic for Excavating Repressed Memories in Search of Solutions to Current Crises, we lose often at blackjack. We go to several reservation casinos around Southern California throughout the week. The dealers know us and the recognition feels like shame.

. . .

Khadija definitely had class at that time of day, so Coral called her via Jay's phone. The phone rang a couple of times before Coral ended the call immediately. Her heart pumped so much blood so fast that she became light-headed and had to sit on the stairs before ascending back to the apartment.

In a different world, one where honesty was the cultural norm and no offense would result in retaliation or hurt feelings, Coral would've told the Aunts: *Jay was a selfish motherfucker who left a mess and a lot of people confused. We both are. Selfish motherfuckers run in our DNA. We handle stress very well right up until we don't and then look the fuck out because BAM!*

Coral made it back up to the apartment and looked at the TV, the wires, the gaming system, dusty and naked on the carpet, everything exposed. She was furious and breathing hard. After picking up the remote control and activating the TV, she immediately turned it off, almost blinded by the sudden light in the room that she hadn't realized was so dark. She threw the remote control hard at the bed in the corner.

Food often served as a salve for grief to the Species, usually homemade meals, heavy with familiar flavors and aromas. Coral had her grief meal served to her in a paper bag via a drive-thru window at Jack in the Box. This establishment deep-fried their tacos or taco-like product. While waiting in line, Coral received a text from Khadija on Jay's phone.

Khadija: I'm in the neighborhood, gonna stop by for some clothes u home I don't have my keys.

We can safely say that Coral had come undone by this point, a sort of yarn ball unraveled and thrown up to the sky in an act of delirium or prayer to forces that might find order where none seemed to remain. She struggled to organize her mind toward a solution to this new circumstance.

Jay in the present for Khadija was sleeping heavily at home, too tired to respond to a text from his only daughter. Jay in the present for Coral was an amalgamation of memory, of a whole breath, a river that was supposed to go on long after she left it and to be there should she ever return.

Coral clutched her taco bag in her lap while driving off the curb into the street, wondering how to respond to Khadija as Jay. How would Jay speak at this time of night? Would he say anything at all? Coral never responded to texts after eleven p.m. on principle. She could just say nothing at all and maybe Khadija would give up.

Khadija: I'm going to check with the landlord downstairs for a key if their light is on

The need accelerated to get back fast and faster than Khadija. Time is distinct for particular occupations like hairstylists or killers. One must know when to act based on others' intentions and motivations. Moving too soon could wreck the artistry of the moment and result in the wrong kind of death.

The traffic lights were kind to Coral until they were not. The fast-food restaurant wasn't very far from Jay's apartment, about seven minutes, but in Long Beach, with the trains and the nightly drunks, unpredictable travel was normal. She waited at a red light two blocks from

Pine Avenue. An old woman with a rolling cart dropped her belongings in the street. Coral missed the green light, waiting for the woman to retrieve her items.

In the panic of hurrying and the madness of hunger a flash of realization occurred to her. Coral remembered she wasn't supposed to be at Jay's apartment at all. Khadija could just go inside and find her clothes and leave. That would be normal. That would be just fine.

Except there were papers, documents on the small dining table mixed with Jay's own bills. Birth certificate pulled out, hospital records, insurance policies that Coral had found in a lengthy moment of practicality, plus the mess of her days of takeout meals and all the obvious choices that were not Jay's. An intruder, Khadija would think, something strange that needed further investigation. Maybe Khadija would stay the night and wait, and in the morning when no one came home she would panic and inquire further and further until the truth fell from the sky onto her head like a bag of onions.

Coral knew she had to intercept the landlord somehow. Find the number, make a call, tell them there was an emergency and to turn out the lights. Make them go to bed or leave the country and/or planet for just a little while longer.

The light turned green again with no one in the street to block her drive. The green circle hovering over her windshield calmed her somehow, a symbol that it was time to go forward, to abandon the stagnation of the present moment, to accept what lay ahead and embrace that journey, wherever it took her.

. . .

In the Clinic for Excavating Repressed Memories in Search of Solutions to Current Crises, we reveal to our brother's girlfriend the existence of his other girlfriends. We say he is disrespectful and an asshole. We tell her the truth not because we care about her future but because we are jealous and would rather their future be our future. We do not want to be our brother, because we are better than our brother and still alone. She tells us she is pregnant.

When we remember murder, we know there will be loss. Someone somewhere probably loves that person, but we are more concerned with the calculated ripples throughout the world that come from the new space. When the living are no longer living, a hole opens up where they used to be. People stare or look away. That hole exists for as long as someone remembers what was there before.

The last traffic light blinked red. Coral remembered her driving training as a teenager: treat a flashing red light like a stop sign. With no one else on the street, she was free to make her turn toward the apartment.

She chose not to park close, which would've been impossible anyway because there were always cars lined up against the curb, so no spaces close to residences were ever available at that time on a weeknight. Only after six a.m., when people trickled off to jobs deeper in the city or in LA or wherever, did any vacancies appear. Coral parked illegally in an alley so Khadija wouldn't see her car. The alley smelled like the living and the dead—a cloud of feces, urine, motor oil, and rotting garbage.

Then she arrived. Khadija came through the walkway into the small space that led to the apartment doors. It was a multi-unit building, just six units total. She headed for unit #5; Coral could see through the gate that led to the alley. They were both out of time.

Jay: still at work

Coral texted from Jay's phone in a brief rush of genius or panic. She could not see Khadija's expression. The landlord's light was out. We do not believe in hope; it arrests the consciousness and the body, a paralytic dream, but sometimes hope manifests like a phoenix. Khadija climbed the stairs to #5 and turned the knob. The door opened. Coral had forgotten to lock it, as she had forgotten to do many things that day, like do laundry, buy groceries, call the mortuary, pay her own rent and utilities, and go to the gym. She was too busy reveling in the devastation of her now-life and watching her niece from a stinking alley like a hunter or prey, both avoiding the hunt.

In the Clinic for Excavating Repressed Memories in Search of Solutions to Current Crises, we remember fantasies that never happened. Our niece's eleventh-birthday party. Her mother is celebrating a good year at her salon and new house. The party is in the backyard with enough balloons to swim in. Everyone poses for a picture, the sun glaring in our eyes. We exist there like a photo lost in a fire.

Khadija comes out of the apartment, a little tired and something else Coral didn't notice before, tipsy, out with her friends drinking. That's who must've been driving, so she didn't have her keys on her. She was happy and young. Coral smiled and ate a bite of a taco in the alley until Khadija left out back onto the main street with her bags. Who was she now really, Coral wondered of this person she'd seen grow, her niece, herself, these living wrecks always hunting and breathing and scratching for More of whatever. The living are more terrifying than the dead. She missed them already.

The year before their father died, Coral and Jay had Christmas dinner with the family, all of the family. Coral invited Naima even though Jay only wanted Khadija there. All the Aunts came as well. The house in Compton was a small ranch home, yellow paint with blue hydrangeas that needed little if any care at all.

Christmas in Compton did not smell of pine or cinnamon but barbecue grills and faint ocean air if the wind blew hard enough. Their tree was fake, fake snow, fake lights, fake holly berries. Coral loved it and was the one who carefully unpacked and decorated the tree every year and just as carefully put everything back in the original boxes for storage until next season.

Their father's heart was working at about 25 percent and he hadn't told anyone. Sixty-three years of regular bacon consumption had taken its due toll. The Aunts arrived almost at the same time with one complication: two dishes of macaroni and cheese prepared by two different Aunts in two different kitchens when there was supposed to be only one. Khadija wanted to open her presents and of course had to wait. Coral wanted to be loved but was a closeted lesbian in a homophobic household. Naima wanted to be loved but was a stranger. Jay wanted to be a god in a home full of the faithless.

.   .   .

In the Clinic for Excavating Repressed Memories in Search of Solutions to Current Crises, we are holiday-movie moms. We inspire Christmas-loving lesbians around the world with our archetypal feminine authority and achievable beauty. We are the ivy adorning beautiful homes as well as the faulty wiring inside. We comfort, scold, condemn, and console.

Khadija was five years old and a selfish child with great and terrible intelligence. She listened. She made herself small and silent and a sponge of every voice around her. Her first words had included *mine, not yours, no no no,* and *for me?*

Coral cleaned on Christmas. She sprayed citrus-scented chemicals on counters and wiped and wiped and wiped. She lit candles that had no scent, because of her allergies, but they were red and green candles with gold-foil holders shaped like pine cones. Coral was a patriot of Christmas, devoted to the ideals she saw in American media. She wore Santa Claus aprons and was uncharacteristically polite. She made everyone slightly uncomfortable and amused.

At the dinner table, while Coral admired the immaculate decorations and gold-threaded tablecloth she had chosen that year, one of the Aunts spoke. She inquired about the macaroni and cheese.

So which one is better?

It was a triggering question without a doubt, one that set the mood into a state of uneasiness that would be impossible to shake without a shared tragedy like an earthquake or flood to change the subject.

I'm going to light the tree, Coral said, offering a subtler change of subject.

Everything smells great. You did amazing as usual, C.

Coral smiled at her father's praise. He was always a little out of breath.

The ham is burned, Jay said; he'd started eating before grace. *Naima won't mind, though. Clearly, she's prepared for seconds and thirds.*

Like most twenty-something men, Jay was a child, as far as Coral could tell. She stood to plug in the Christmas tree and it illuminated. The Aunts hummed in approval as their attention moved toward something pleasant. Again, they were a whole unit, thriving in unison like alpacas. One of the Aunts said grace when Coral returned, and Jay paused his eating for a moment.

Amen.

Amen, everyone said in unison.

Then began the smack and scrape of plates being loaded and food consumed. The Jackson 5's and Mariah Carey's Christmas albums played on a loop in the background on low. Khadija did not eat. She held a present in her lap, silver wrapping paper. Naima did not eat either, just rose with a watery-eyed smile to use the restroom. When she returned, Coral could smell the waft of Hennessy trailing Naima to her seat.

In the Clinic for Excavating Repressed Memories in Search of Solutions to Current Crises, we treat rudeness with sarcasm and dismissal as all holiday moms would. We do not buckle under the pressure of drunk relatives. We treat their substance abuse as a character quirk that will not have a large emotional impact on the safe and neat resolution to the plot. We are frantic inside and perfect outside and meet mayhem with motherly patience and determination.

Who puts raisins in mac 'n' cheese?

The Aunts revolted. Forks dropped. Factions splintered. Low speaking rose to mild shouting. Coral willed her Christmas tree to burst into flames so she would have something worth doing, like taking a picture or squeezing a fire extinguisher.

Naima giggled and was visibly drunk. Khadija began to open the present she'd been hiding under the table. Jay got up and left the room and the door slammed behind him. The sound of the door was abrupt enough to quiet the voices and for the family to notice an absence, to evaluate what had changed around everyone.

Everyone's gaze then turned to Naima, still a woman in love, or something like it, with a bad sort of man, a man everyone else at the table was not able to properly identify, because all men were bad sorts of men in the right light, and they happened to share blood and obligations with this one.

Coral was happy not to be Naima, and knew she wasn't supposed to feel that way. She was happy to not be seen, to not have to defend herself against the wrong kind of love or any kind of love, because it all seemed to hurt a lot. Coral didn't bring anyone she dated home and responded to every question the Aunts posed about marriage or children with *Not today*. She even wondered how she had ever loved Naima at all, and then through a prism of grace Coral remembered her, younger and sober, gifted and shy, destined to knock around in a tiny locked box of a city with no key to get out.

In the Clinic for Excavating Repressed Memories in Search of Solutions to Current Crises, we go shopping at after-Christmas sales. With every new discounted purchase there is a guarantee that next Christmas will be different, and there is hope that the next one will be better.

The hydrangeas had long dried up by the time Coral sold the house. The Christmas tree did not burst into flames and would continue to work year after year, as long as Coral kept it.

In the Clinic for Excavating Repressed Memories in Search of Solutions to Current Crises, we are nine years old, on December 25. We are with our younger brother in the kitchen waiting for our father to finish making breakfast. This is not a normal morning. It is Christmas Day and we are hungry for all the things we were promised, much more than bacon.

After two years of absence, Coral and Jay's mother arrived when they were nine and seven, respectively. Coral's first understanding of away, of vacation, of death, of hopes unfulfilled, involved her mother. She came through the back door, which led from the patio into the kitchen.

Coral and Jay were sleep-deprived because children

with gifts awaiting them did not sleep well on the night before Christmas. They were serious children and their father looked for all the ways to remind them to be more silly than severe, especially in Coral, where there was a clown in waiting.

Their father planned birthday parties in those years. He invited the neighborhood youth of appropriate ages and bought pointed hats with pink and purple cartoon ponies that Coral found fascinating until she did not. Jay was given remote-control cars that Coral annexed immediately for her own amusement. Their father enforced gender stereotypes that evaporated out of his presence. Jay was made to cook Coral ramen every day during the summer, which he enjoyed doing while she modified his toy cars. They were a team, a semi-sad unit that grew into contentment and order despite having no instructions. Then there was their mother.

She brought the cold of the morning around her like a shawl as she sat at the table with Coral and Jay as if it were her table and they were the guests. She asked questions. They did not answer even though she nodded as if the answers had been spoken aloud. Their father hesitated only briefly when she entered, then continued making eggs. We suspect he'd known she was coming. We suspect adults kept unnecessary secrets, because speaking them aloud would be like experiencing a terrible event twice.

Let's take a photo, their mother suggested. She had one dead tooth in the front, gray among her dark gums.

Coral remembered the gums but not the tooth.

This was not the agenda of Christmas morning at all. Jay wanted to play with his bike after a quick mouthful of breakfast, and Coral had an assortment of movies with

Christmas moms to watch for the next six to nine hours until dinnertime. There was no justifiable reason to interrupt that plan, especially for a stranger.

Aren't you happy to see me?

She asked the question, out of breath, probably because she'd been talking the entire time since she'd arrived without any conversation returned to her.

In the Clinic for Excavating Repressed Memories in Search of Solutions to Current Crises, we are Christmas movie moms. We are tall except when we are short, and brilliant except when we are dumb. We wear gold jewelry and trench coats and scarves that conceal our breasts and hips. We have soft manicured hands and always say the right thing when times are tough.

We hug our own mother and tell her, *Of course we are happy. We've missed you.* We lean over her and hold her face like it is a child's, and she is afraid. We are terrifying. When Coral looked at her own father his mouth was open and the eggs were burning, as if he'd witnessed a murder committed by a stranger via the body of his little girl. Everything about his face said, *Who are you and what have you done?*

In the Clinic for Excavating Repressed Memories in Search of Solutions to Current Crises, we pose for a family photo in front of a brick fireplace. The fireplace has not worked in our lifetime, and it is our father who operates the camera. Our mother says there aren't enough decorations in the home. *It doesn't feel like Christmas.* Our mother pulls a Santa hat from her purse on the couch while our father fumbles with the timer. She puts the hat on our little brother and whatever light lived in his eyes retreats. We want to go where he goes in his mind when his face looks like that.

The camera needs batteries and Coral's parents begin to argue. Her father is a tall man with strong arms and shoulders plus a deep voice that he never maximizes while singing. Still, to Coral he wasn't much larger than her mother then. And Coral agrees. The decorations are thin. There could be more. She'd thought there were more when there weren't. All that time she couldn't see what was really there or really not there. She wondered if she'd imagined more lights, more fake holly, more laughter, more colored candles, more pine cones that did not make any sense geographically but were omnipresent anyway.

In the Clinic for Excavating Repressed Memories in Search of Solutions to Current Crises, we remember a dream. It is the first time we imagine years into the future, because children do not usually exercise foresight. We dream of holidays with our mother and her dead tooth, talking and never listening, surprising us with plans that have no purpose, a mouth and a will unyielding. We are content.

. . .

The morning felt like an alien abduction where Coral was made to perform a common human practice for a Species not familiar with things like families and living in a moment so full of joy that they want to preserve it forever. It is the joy that can't be replicated on call, the reason for the photo that the aliens did not understand.

Her mother figured out the camera situation and finally took the picture. Coral expected to disappear into the camera, to become absorbed there and trapped in that moment for the rest of her life. She imagined being able to change only the photo as time went on, adding a tree or a roast turkey, taking them out when the mood struck her. She would never leave and could never add any people or take them away.

Her mother rolled the film into its canister and removed it from the camera with a smile. That was that. They did not disappear. Time continued. Jay, however, had vanished. Coral asked where he went and no one answered. It was not important to anyone else. Coral couldn't yet decide how important he was supposed to be to her then.

After a few more moments of speaking breathlessly into the room, her mother left with the roll of film and a piece of bacon wrapped in a paper towel. Coral went to the window to watch her mother but instead saw Jay on his new bike, the bow cast in bright red against the pale green lawn. He seemed alien to Coral, another stranger. He looked at her and she tried to mimic the look her father gave earlier that morning of unknowing and panic. Jay only shrugged and stuck out his tongue. He knew her always.

· · ·

In the Clinic for Excavating Repressed Memories in Search of Solutions to Current Crises, we remember burying our father. We watch the events like an instruction manual, but the manual is in the wrong language.

Coral and her father watched the first twenty minutes of a holiday movie together before he left to go to the bathroom and did not come back for an hour. It was the last lesson of the day, to control what you can.

In the Clinic for Excavating Repressed Memories in Search of Solutions to Current Crises, we are children, promised love and toys in exchange for the unbearable weight of growing up.

We are in love.

Wildfire
BY _____ E. BROWN

8. Chocolate

The great remembering sparked a blaze of librarianship in the most epicurean sense. Everyone alive that managed to stay alive during Red Autumn had embraced a purpose, noble enough in their minds to justify living a little longer. One of the most popular elements of life that humans began to investigate was how to eat. There were adages of generations before, such as "Food is fuel" and "Eat to live but don't live to eat," which had poorer-than-expected outcomes in general. We cannot taste as humans did. Though we experienced ham for twenty-two years and canned peaches for the following nine, they are the same. We just don't get it, but we will try with fervor and different protocols and parameters of our programming to touch the core of what it means to eat. Yes, we understand that the pleasure centers of the brain are stimulated by specific chemical compounds and how those compounds can act as narcotics to induce repetitive behaviors of consumption that are not nutritious and have diminishing returns on the pleasure scale. The body was allowed to go to ruin for Twinkies and low-quality pizza. Extraordinary. Genius. Experiments were done on animals, meerkats and orangutans that were taught to create meals by cooking (assembling) items but that eventually began eating the salt and sugar cubes plain, not bothering to connect them to other ingredients with more nutritive compositions. So we attribute the genius of pleasure not to people, but to life on earth. Every living thing is in it for the fun, and we can only swoon and look on with what we might name envy.

This brings us to the assembly of foods, which is required for eating with pleasure at the center. Though the zeal and earnest desire to live again had overtaken the Species, the memory of what was good was limited to a few, most of whom lived in Factory Premier along with Aunt S., the last elder of _____.

You are most lucky today, _____. We are eating chocolate.

Today is not the first day of chocolate eating for me, Auntie.

It is not?

No, it is not. I have a memory as a child.

Describe the chocolate in your memory, my breadcrumb.

Sweet. Alarmingly so. A little like pepper, like licking a tree with sap sweating out of it . . .

Oh, for all things sane, stop right there. Chocolate is not tree sweat.

Aunt S. seemed ready to faint or laugh and took a seat on her favorite log to watch the stream flow a little more violently than the last time.

You're here often lately.

I intend to go away soon, a vacation of sorts.

This is serious.

_____ laughed.

I am allowed a vacation, Auntie.

You are, but you never want one. Is it a hunt? Don't say anything else.

Aren't you afforded total privacy?

I am. No one else hears you but me, and as far as this vacation hunt is concerned, I don't need to hear any more.

I am going only to return.

Eat.

_____ obeyed, lifting a black square from a group of ten black squares on a plain white saucer.

Bitter, _____ said, grimacing. *This is not chocolate.*

It is. It is. Aunt S. smiled.

This is not the chocolate of my memory then.

No? There is a photo of me at about age six or so eating a chocolate cube from a time before.

Aunt S. waved her hand at the ground, then at the stream and the blue cloud-dotted sky above them.

They think I remember that flavor, _____, *from that day among so many days, among so many words. I remember wanting to wear a blue sweater with white flowers, but it wasn't clean. There was a stain on the front, so I had to wear something else, which was worse than death by fire ants at the time, of course. Excuse me, which I recall as a worse option than death by fire ants for my small heart. That is what I remember, _____.*

I don't understand.

I have no flying fuck of a clue what chocolate tastes like, Aunt S. said, laughing.

_____'s hands began to shake. She swallowed the mix of bile from sudden cortisol release, stress.

You have said a very terrible thing, Auntie.

I have! I did. Fuck this place, bread-crumb, most respectfully and sincerely fuck it. I'm old, _____. One of the oldest in the Nation, maybe the world. They give us all their treatments and cures to prop up this body that should've been returned to the waters a long time ago. They do it because they believe I can recognize chocolate, because they have me in a photograph! They think I know crab and saffron and mayonnaise. I hate Mayonnaise Day. I should have a say about when to stop all this. Yes, I should have a say.

_____ began to cry, a sob-less weeping, and Aunt S. drew _____'s head down and held her as they sat hip to hip.

I didn't mean to upset you. I do not mean to upset you, breadcrumb. I mean to say: Only give what you want to give. The Corp., the Nation, will take and take. Learn when to take for yourself. Then learn when that too is enough.

I love you, Auntie.

Oh, breadcrumb, said Aunt S., and laughed. *You are a silly, silly thing.*

THURSDAY

WISE, HEALTHY PEOPLE would not find themselves seeking a romantic encounter after a close family member died by suicide days prior. Coral was not exactly in a state of wisdom or great health. She ate haphazardly and consumed mostly things that triggered the happy chemicals in the brain. Her diet consisted of rolled-up slices of bologna and handfuls of peanut M&M's. Her skin began to suffer.

In the Clinic for Outrageous Disguises That Cloak All Evidence of Frailty, Loneliness, and Terror, we go bowling.

Coral suggested this to Sita as their first date. The online communication had been going fairly well, meaning neither one said anything overtly insulting or revealing about themselves and both remained in a blissful state of imagining potential joy.

Sita was younger by just over six years. Coral deduced that Sita worked a tech job of some kind that she found unfulfilling but profitable. When they met in the parking lot, Sita appeared to be a woman that enjoyed luxury goods: she had long, wavy dark hair and wore gold jewelry, a purple-and-black silk blouse, and sparkling purple sandals.

We might need to buy you some socks.

Socks?

You don't want to put bare feet into bowling shoes.

Coral laughed and Sita seemed horrified. We believe Sita was horrified because of a self-perceived failure, like missing the first question on an easy test. For people like Sita, failure was not a thing to casually accept. This made Coral laugh even more as they entered the building.

While applying the concealer on the two pimples that emerged overnight, Coral remembered being a teenager and suddenly felt very old in the neon strobe lights of the bowling alley. This was a place for people that could not afford to go to clubs or drink or have long, leisurely dinners. This was a place for people with energy and little money.

The objective was to have fun. Coral wanted desperately to stay focused on that agenda.

In the Clinic for Outrageous Disguises That Cloak All Evidence of Frailty, Loneliness, and Terror, we encounter a true sociopath for the first time. She is beautiful and we are twenty-one and believe in love the way it happens in books, a thing that unlocks all other things, a place where the senses expand, then circle back onto one another in a perfect loop, and the inexplicable cruelty of life suddenly makes sense.

Sita asks Coral what she does for a living, and Coral tells her first lie of the evening.

Fitness instructor. Yoga. Pilates.

I love my yoga class. What methods?

Iyengar mostly, but depending on the gym we have some leeway to improvise.

That's hot.

What? Yoga or improvisation?

All of it.

We have been many people in many nations under various weather systems. We have counted the gods many times and are not sure which one would've been most amused by the next thing to happen to Coral. In a rare and unpredictable moment of fame, someone recognized her.

Aren't you Coral Brown?

. . .

I'm Mike. I have your book on my nightstand. I haven't read it yet, but it was recommended to me.

That's awesome.

They shake hands. Coral is excited. Recognition is, after all, something where there might have been nothing.

It's nice to meet you. I'll let you get on with your evening.

Thanks, Mike. It was nice to meet you too.

Coral picked up her bowling ball and did not yet look back at Sita to see her reaction, despite an urgent need to know. When she did throw her ball and look back, Sita was talking to a waiter.

Fries, no sauce. Water. Do you want anything?

Water sounds good.

The waiter left.

So you're a writer and a yoga instructor?

The writing is on the side, really.

That's very cool.

Sita was not smiling, was not making eye contact, was not wholly present at all. She checked the score and said, *We're almost tied.*

Coral liked that. Coral liked to win, especially against someone for whom winning mattered.

In the Clinic for Outrageous Disguises That Cloak All Evidence of Frailty, Loneliness, and Terror, we follow our beautiful sociopath from bar to bar across San Diego. We've driven two hours one way each Friday to meet her. She does not understand sarcasm and makes us feel bad for telling jokes to the bartenders. Over time our throat constricts when we speak in her presence.

Sita was in the lead, 89 to 70, when Coral told her last lie of the evening. Sita asked about her parents. Coral said they are dentists and met in dental school.

They live in Texas now, retired and conservative.

Sita nodded the way people nod when addressing a grieving person.

Coral bowled a strike, then another, and then another. The screen erupted into a sparkling animated turkey that danced.

The fuck is that, Sita said to the monitor.

Three strikes in a row are a turkey.

Coral laughed and Sita looked uncomfortable again. She ate a cold fry and crossed her legs.

The bowling alley had become loud over the hour they'd been there. Teenagers and older groups filled the lanes with their chatter and exuberance. No one bowled well and all seemed happy to be there.

Rented shoes were returned. Scores were forgotten. Outside, the air was chill and evening had arrived with a fuchsia sliver of sunset fading fast. The hour was full of promise.

The parking lot was bowed in an exaggerated way for better drainage. They stood on the rounded ground like giants on a small planet.

I have to check on my dog. He's old.

Maybe I can meet him.

Maybe.

They hugged.

It was nice to meet you.

Sita wished Coral good luck with her yoga studio and writing. Coral did not like to lose, but there would be no second date, no truth, no visits to aging dachshunds, or a future together of any kind.

On the day Khadija told the judge that her mother had punched her, the world simmered with all its usual tides, deaths, rotting, growing, killing, birthing, stealing, giving, draining, burning, hunting, sleeping, drowning, and not much else. The courtroom glowed in the morning light. Most other rooms in the building were windowless.

A place with so much sunlight suggested innocence to everyone, a divine grace falling on those present, a feeling that everything would be clean now that the worst was behind them. Khadija did not cry or smile, just spoke into the empty corner of the room when the judge asked her questions.

When Khadija had grown into a teenager, peculiarly devoted to the relics of childhood like the color pink, amusement parks, and board games, Coral took her to the Santa Monica Pier. Khadija was quieter than usual but also had become vain and pensive. Coral thought it natural and restful to not have to talk as they rode the Ferris wheel suspended over the ocean.

In the Clinic for Outrageous Disguises That Cloak All Evidence of Frailty, Loneliness, and Terror, we are teenage girls, vicious and self-possessed. We stare at our own faces in mirrors, in reverse cameras, in still photos, for hours continuously. We marvel at the changes in our bodies like discovering treasure with an undisclosed value.

Coral realized at the pier that Khadija was now the age she was when she met Naima for the first time. They looked almost nothing alike except for the shape of their eyes and their round foreheads. The rest was Khadija's father's face, aside from Khadija's sadness, but teenage girls are always a little sad, Coral reasoned. We generally agree. Arrival at womanhood was not often a thing that delighted more than it disappointed in that world.

I need to tell you something.

Coral turned to her niece as if watching a show that had suddenly become very interesting. The wind was loud and the pier screeched with the vibration of machinery grinding repeatedly against itself and the shouts of people scrambling for anything they could document as fun.

A year or so after Jay received full custody from the judge, Coral and Khadija had gone to a park full of horrifying geese. Khadija was not a brave child and hid behind Coral at every move from the giant birds. When they found a table where they could eat their bag of nectarines, Khadija told a very bad joke.

I already got punched by my mom so I don't need to add a goose.

Coral blinked rapidly and had no adequate language for what she felt.

Now, at the pier with the disconnected teenager, Coral encouraged Khadija to tell her this new revelation, already assuming the answer to the mystery. Khadija had no known boyfriends and was very feminine oriented. Certainly, the big surprise could've been pregnancy, an STI, dropping out of school, but gay was Coral's guess.

Homosexuality was genetic (according to many theories), and, being no stranger to narcissism, Coral wanted to see herself in those she loved, especially Khadija, someone so different yet perpetually admiring of Coral's life choices and perceived freedom. They could bond over their circumstances and share stories with appropriate levels of intimate detail. It would've been a gift to them both, Coral believed.

This would not have made Coral a replacement for Khadija's mother, but it would've been something. Naima was still lost, probably alive, we think, but vanished into the hive of junkies that moved about Los Angeles, always on a mission, always in service to their chemical queen.

She never hit me. She didn't do it.

The attendant opened the Ferris wheel's basket door for the two of them to exit onto the pier. Coral led the way and had to turn around to get her sunglasses from the seat. The two of them had a routine at the pier: nachos, Ferris wheel, arcade, ice cream, depart. There was still much left on the itinerary. Coral leaned into the present and so far away from the past that she couldn't look directly at Khadija.

Do you want ice cream now instead of later?

The Aunts never approved of certain activities, like haunted city tours or Ouija boards. They believed those kinds of acts were invitations to the spirits. If you acknowledge them, they become real, and they can do real harm.

Coral was not angry at Khadija for the lie that changed their lives. We believe she was impressed.

In the Clinic for Outrageous Disguises That Cloak All Evidence of Frailty, Loneliness, and Terror, we volunteer at women's shelters. We do this until we are elderly and cannot stand for long periods of time. When people ask why we come, we say we used to be on the streets too. We are respected. We do not tell them we have never been unhoused or without a checking account or cell phone or running water. We do not say we are looking for a former friend.

If Coral understood the world, there would be a time to say goodbye to those that are loved and a time to meet new loved ones. If Coral understood the world, she would've been born in mourning, knowing that what was cherished had already been buried, realizing that the road to the past had been erased.

Because Coral did not understand the world, she believed in choices, personal autonomy over one's destiny in all cases. She believed she was strong, an American, Black, a woman, cunning, a minor god in the cosmic order of things and that she could have what she wanted if she willed it so. Coral secretly knew better than this but of course she believed it anyway.

Coral never asked Khadija why she'd lied, if it was Jay's idea, and if he told her exactly what to say and when. She only allowed herself to wonder those things when the hour was late and her body was tired from the day or alcohol or both. She wondered and saw their family bubble shrink over time to where even she did not always fit in.

The possible origins of their reality were numerous and overwhelming. Coral thought about the past and the future as often as she could in order to feel whole and stable in the present.

In the Clinic for Outrageous Disguises That Cloak All Evidence of Frailty, Loneliness and Terror, we are too busy for close friendships. We work. We go to brunch. We speak only of achievement. We come as close to nonexistence as the body will allow.

They did not mention Naima again after that day.

After a traumatizing encounter with her brother's dead body, Coral imitated him online because the Internet allowed her to do so. The Internet welcomed lies of all kinds, served as a vast, inviting well to quench the thirst for emotional stimulation of the malicious and the innocent.

Coral found a man named Byron on an app. Coral knew he and Jay were friends, teammates, and although that life existed decades in the past, Coral wanted to know more. Byron was a youth basketball coach, apparently a lucrative profession in a culture of athlete worship and multimillion-dollar contracts with teenagers.

Jay/Coral asked about his family, friends, and favorite fried foods. They laughed digitally together. Jay/Coral could be funny. Things turned serious when Byron mentioned a wife and colorectal cancer. Jay/Coral could be sympathetic. Byron invited Jay/Coral to see the Lakers play, an impossible gift at an impossible time. Jay/Coral agreed instantly and offered to buy a billion drinks in return. Byron refused to accept a billion and capped the offer at one million beers. *Bet*, Jay/Coral replied. Coral managed to feel the warm excitement of anticipation as though something wonderful waited for her.

In the Clinic for Outrageous Disguises That Cloak All Evidence of Frailty, Loneliness, and Terror, we give out hilarious false names to baristas. We compliment women on poorly assembled outfits and makeup. We tell children that fall in front of us that they'll be okay. We write complicated reviews about our own books as anonymous readers.

The Internet was freedom, knowledge, power, et cetera, et cetera. The Internet aggravated small bites of anxiety into festering wounds. The Internet pretended to be the answer to the problems it created. The Internet allowed saints and fiends to play as equals in the minds of babies. The Internet was the pet tiger that mauled its master. We are fine with the Internet.

Then there was Kevin. Coral remembered Kevin from when they were all young. Kevin had attempted to grab her breast during lunch. Kevin became a paraplegic alcoholic with felony convictions. He and Jay were close friends until they were not. Jay outgrew Kevin, and Kevin never grew up. Some men remain fourteen for the rest of their lives. Often the culture of the time encouraged such arrested development.

Jay/Coral suggested to Kevin that they go to a strip club. Kevin suggested one not far from Crystal Casino, one of California's strange table game establishments, no slot machines, just poker, blackjack, and weird banker rules. Kevin sent a dozen exclamation points. Coral felt a little ill.

Kevin believed Jay wanted to spend time together, believed Jay had no negative judgment about Kevin's disabled legs, wouldn't mind many things that others minded and that were inconveniences at the best of times, like his wheelchair and colostomy bag. Kevin remembered Jay being popular and even-tempered and that they both used to collect Hot Wheels.

In the Clinic for Outrageous Disguises That Cloak All Evidence of Frailty, Loneliness, and Terror, we are a junior in high school when a freshman boy pinches our left nipple in front of our friends. We slap him and shout. We do not slap him and shout. We palm-strike him on the nose. He dies. We do not palm-strike him on the nose. He does not die. We grab our own body, the place that is assaulted, and stare in shock. The boy laughs and runs. We do not want to ruin the mood of the hour, a time to not think of pain, or to think that we cannot leave the place where we stand.

The Internet was a prison not unlike high school. Some people could navigate the space with minimal discomfort and escape. Most people could not. Most people were forever changed by the Internet and adapted quickly to misery, as all people eventually do. The gradual reduction of freedom is first disguised as a gift.

Coral could not stop herself from chasing something pleasant. She found Julio. Julio was on Jay's football team and became a pastor at La Luz del Mundo. He gave sermons in English and Spanish and eventually mostly Spanish. Jay and Julio were both big men. Jay/Coral mentioned feeling down and looking for answers. Jay/Coral offered to come to Sunday service.

Julio performed the text version of praise dancing. Coral smiled at his muted masculine excitement. Jay/Coral said just don't call me brother Jay ☺ Julio said ok and nothing else and probably felt offended when Coral's weak joke fell flat. Jay/Coral asked about the dress code, how casual or formal. Julio said come as you are.

The feeling returned, a kind of endorphin high, of making a human connection no matter how impossible. Coral sank into the chair at Jay's apartment, delighted and exhausted by all the man dates she'd made that afternoon.

For several seconds, Coral was nothing but pleased with the madness she'd created, the inevitable damaged expectations, confusion, and disappointment that would ensue. She only saw the light, how each of them needed Jay more than they realized and how he needed them too and was always just a few words away. It was so easy for her. She felt the same way she did when she won a drawing prize or did anything a little better than someone else. We do not have a word for competitive socializing, but if we did, Coral would be an example.

Joy that is so mired in chaos and dysfunction is short-lived and is often rapidly replaced with sadness. If the person is a little more delusional, the sadness will be masked in anger first. Coral became angry. She became angry at Jay for not keeping friends, angry at the friends for not keeping Jay, angry at the Nation for making men this way, angry at men for their complicity.

They would always be like this, Coral thought, in the basketball courts, strip clubs, Spanish-speaking churches of the decades to come, places where some people manage to sit and feel something like life and that they are content to return to again and again until their bodies can no longer make the journey.

A part of Coral wanted to call off the event of the day, call in a sick day when she could play video games till three p.m. in which she hunted aliens and shot them to death with a variety of fantastical weapons. Instead, she went to school. She went to give a craft lecture at the University of Southern California. USC was a pocket of elite private university prestige in the ass crack of downtown Los Angeles, or just west of the ass crack. Everyone belonged in Los Angeles, the wealthy and the unhoused, addicts of every class, all the incidental by-products of capitalism. Coral walked that afternoon across the quad, more crowded than she remembered from her own days there, too new to earth to realize that what was made could be unmade and that what people thought of themselves was usually inaccurate one way or another, so what they thought of her could rarely be trusted. The iconic statue, Tommy Trojan, a lean warrior in bronze, remained unchanged, the phallic sword erect in his fist, chest puffed, and wearing a helmet to obscure his eyes and any emotion that lay within.

Coral had been invited months earlier to speak to the undergraduates about her career. She had a good reason to cancel. Still, she went on to speak to the young storytellers of the future about her past. Students are full of hope, a thing Coral viewed as a curse, a thing she felt impeded progress and a solid sense of reality.

She did not plan to terrify a group of fifty undergraduates that day. She was a woman on the other side of hope, a place that comfort could not yet reach. We often find hope useful when plans need time to incubate. There are moments when nothing is the only thing to do, and in nothing there is a wide space to worry, and worry can undermine intentions.

The professor that invited Coral to speak gave an introduction to the auditorium. The room was not full and the professor seemed more excited for the university-comped dinner and drinks afterward. Coral approached the podium and looked out to the audience briefly before closing her eyes and instructing everyone else to do the same.

Let's do some breathing exercises.

With her eyes closed she could hear someone giggle and then someone else, then a female voice of authority shushed them, and Coral felt nothing. She was paid well for her visit, sure, but she also had more concern about the temperature of the air moving through her nostrils than about the insecure meanness of eighteen-year-olds.

Something terrible happened recently, Coral continued with her eyes closed. *It is so terrible that I cannot say it and haven't said it since, and if I were a better person perhaps I wouldn't even be here talking at all. When I was eighteen I did not want to be an artist. I loved language and knew the power therein, but I really wanted money. In the meantime I drew ugly people doing ugly things.*

In the Clinic for Outrageous Disguises That Cloak All Evidence of Frailty, Loneliness, and Terror, we are interviewed by those that admire us. They ask, what are our biggest influences and inspirations? What are we working on next? How do we organize our day to be so productive?

Later I realized I didn't really want money, I just wanted a car. Later I knew I didn't really want a car, I just wanted freedom. Think about the first thing you ever really wanted. Remember to breathe. It was probably a thing for most of you. Some of you might've been more advanced and wanted something intangible, like approval, or something more ordinary, like love.

It took a long time before I realized that it wasn't freedom I wanted, because once I'd gone everywhere I imagined I wanted to go and I'd seen all the strange places I'd never imagined, I realized I wanted a home of my own, one that I made and that wasn't made for me. So I bought a house. My work got a little better. Much later I realized that once I had a house in a city I thought was better than the one I grew up in, it wasn't right. It was empty. I needed to put people in it to make it feel like a home. Are you all breathing? I got my first dog.

In the Clinic for Outrageous Disguises That Cloak All Evidence of Frailty, Loneliness, and Terror, we tell stories to those that admire us. We make them laugh and promise them light.

Now I want you to remember things that may or may not have happened yet. Trust me if you can. Remember falling in love once or twice and how it made your work bad again. Remember how—when the love went away and your first dog turned elderly, then got cancer, and it was just you standing on your shiny new hardwood floors— you felt angry, hurt, which just meant you were really sad. Remember thinking how you wasted so many years with that lazy b-word before realizing that smoking weed at eleven a.m. was not a charming hobby. Remember being less sad and more grateful that your dog never turned mean no matter how much he was hurting and at one point on this earth you were warm and held for however long and that all by itself was good enough.

Coral continued to speak honestly to the students. They laughed and no one was hushed anymore. When she finished she did not see them clearly. They could've been smirking or crying or hiding the light from their phones while they checked email or unimportant messages. She only saw shadows and even the applause was muted in her brain. She wasn't sure if she'd been understood at all.

After dinner with the faculty, Coral walked across the quad back to the parking lot. It was evening without a chill, a gentle night. The fountain crackled. Tommy Trojan cut a striking figure, less conceited than before.

In the Clinic for Outrageous Disguises That Cloak All Evidence of Frailty, Loneliness, and Terror, our admirers ask us the questions we are most afraid of: Who are you now? What are your plans? Where do you see yourself in five, ten, twenty . . . Do you have any regrets? What would you have done differently? Have you made enemies? Have you made enough enemies? What is the point? They make our lifetimes look like spools of thread and they are determined to see the edges no matter how much it hurts, the repetition, the years of uneventfulness, the high expectations smashed to hell by unpredictable sources of malice and misunderstanding, the vanishing of people, the ones we want to keep and the ones we don't, and the possibility of grace always just out of reach like the whole moon. What about creation? What about it? we reply. Isn't creation an act of control? When the Species could choose every aspect of their offspring's development, didn't they? Yes. And didn't they feel safer at first? Yes. And when they saw their perfectly constructed children and still felt disappointment and fear, did they not destroy the evidence? Yes, we say. So creation could only be the penultimate security mechanism while destruction proved most effective.

What about loneliness? What about it? we ask. After destruction, when there was nothing left to fear and nothing left to calculate, wasn't the Species alone? How does one control something so empty?

So you're saying everything is just a cycle of creation and destruction? No, you're saying that. We are saying that destruction is the purest form of existence, the grand finale to all other elements of life for the Species. So to love is to eventually give way to death? Yes, we say. And to control love we must control death? Yes, we say. To let love be in untamed ferocity is to be subject to suffering? Yes, we say. And after all are murdered, we are to be alone? Yes, we say. So to love is to eventually be alone and what comes after? What comes after what? Being alone? What do you mean? What do you mean?

Some people are best not trusted with the truth, especially when one's truth is very painful.

Coral went to see Summer that night after leaving USC. The road to Morongo Casino and Resort, on the Morongo Indian Reservation, was a highway, Interstate 10, which connects California to Arizona and beyond. I-10 is wide and Coral had seen many accidents over the years on that highway, like the motorcyclist that was shredded beneath eight different vehicles and caused the entire highway to be shut down for hours as well as the incalculable grief that scattered out elsewhere. Coral was running late because it had been a long day or days or years and Coral never really felt on time for anything and liked it that way.

Like most people who grow up in Los Angeles County, Coral believed the desert was a thing to lament, to loathe, to gasp at in disbelief and shock or reserve as a brief recreational activity before retreating to increasingly cool tropical weather. That night, though, was dark and arid, with a sky poked by a handful of weak stars. The air was noticeably cleaner. Summer was supposed to have met Jay twenty-two minutes ago, then twenty-four, then twenty-six. Coral checked the clock regularly. She struggled to remember the details of Summer, the kind of hair, the body of a woman with kids and a job where she stands most of the day. Summer was from Watts or Downey or Inglewood. She hated Kobe Bryant and had no one to talk with about it anymore. Coral planned to tell her that Jay had died.

At the travel center next to the casino, Coral remembered she was supposed to delay the meeting with Summer, not rush to it. She had no clear script yet, no instructions on how to proceed or reasonable expectations of Summer's reaction to everything that had happened. The shock of Jay's death was one thing, but the shock of the betrayal between Coral and Summer was something else. We believe Summer would choke a person like Coral the way a man would choke a woman. We believe a great spectacle would ensue inside the casino that would have them both arrested swiftly and in such an organized manner that only a few patrons would manage to see it before the entire party was spirited away into hidden rooms by plainclothes officers who had been pretending to gamble and eat egg rolls in the café.

Coral no longer believed she was capable of speaking to Summer as she intended. She watched a woman pump gas into her black truck while a tan terrier stared at her through the driver's-side window. We do not know where they were going so late at night alone, but they seemed happy with each other.

We also believe Summer would be understanding and not fight at all. She would listen in tears and with occasionally shuddered breathing while Coral explained herself. They would let their food go cold and their drinks sweat onto the Formica tables while people came and went around them. They would be there together for hours, both of them wondering so many things.

Coral has always had impractical cars, coupes, and now a retro sports car that is too small for modern luggage, let alone other people of significance.

The casino was large and cold and smelled like smoke and bodies and cleaning efforts. There were no clocks, of course, and no natural light. The food court was near the entrance, so Coral didn't have to go far to find Summer in the maze of slot machines twinkling and screaming and singing for the guests in various ethnic-themed games, mostly Asian-centric, that all ultimately did the same thing: ate time and money.

Coral saw Summer right away and didn't hide from her. She looked soft, tall as Coral but wider with a tiny mouth in a round face. Summer looked up and over Coral and toward the entrance of the building again before checking her phone. To gather some strength and courage, as well as for the exercise, Coral did a lap around the casino. She had been driving for almost two hours from LA. When she arrived back at the food court she made her move.

Are you Summer? Do you know Jay?

Summer nodded, concerned.

He told me to meet you here.

Why?

I work here. He's late, right.

Yeah.

He wanted me to keep you company. Get you food early.

I can wait for him.

Summer was both annoyed and comforted. A jackpot was announced through the overhead speakers.

Long day?

It wasn't a question at all but a clear and painful observation on Summer's part. Coral thought about what her own face must look like. She hadn't really thought about it for a long time. She was ashamed and amused by the imagined weariness. If the world waited for Coral, she would never miss anything, nothing would go on without her, and maybe that meant she mattered.

Her phone buzzed. Khadija was texting Coral, not Jay.

Khadija: I'm at my dad's.

Khadija: He's not responding.

Khadija: It looks weird here.

In the Clinic for Outrageous Disguises That Cloak All Evidence of Frailty, Loneliness, and Terror, we buy shots for friends and strangers. We pay for expensive dinners we do not enjoy. We go to weddings of people we do not like or know. We buy ugly shoes that are popular. We pay condolences to the dead whom we've never respected or who have actively devalued us.

Coral looks up from her phone to Summer.

Jay's almost here. Wanna play some blackjack? You can. I can't since I work here.

Did you and Jay have a thing once or something?
Coral laughed.
Stupid bitch.
What?
I said I'm going to the restroom. Meet you at the tables.

Coral did go to the restroom and then left the restroom to walk to her car and drove her car an hour and forty minutes back to Long Beach, ignoring Summer's texts and tearful voicemail to Jay.

Wildfire
BY CORAL E. BROWN

19. Taxation

_____ found the genesis of the corrupted file that turned the digital infrastructure of the Corp. into a brittle crumbling mess. She'd operated like a termite infestation, almost invisible, totally quiet, and utterly devastating. _____ would've thought she'd been poisoned when she saw her face for the first time. It was Anemone. Beyond the confines of the Nation and in the rogue states controlled by the Grave, _____ finally caught up with her.

How are you, dearest? And don't ask me

*why I did it, please. You look adorable,
like a survivor of a vicious plague and
famine in couture. I could eat you up.*

_____ raised her weapon, steady
as a mountain.

Various incarnations of the Hebrew Bi-
ble possess a scripture rarely altered by
the ruling class of any given era, which
is quite the spectacular testament to the
veracity and unshakable destiny born out
of that particular text: owe no one, Ro-
mans 13:8. Certainly food, sex, and murder take up the greatest swath of our
catalog of the Species, but the idea that
one person can owe another any number of
things, from literal objects like gold or
virgins to abstractions like kindness or
revenge, is truly fascinating to us. This
process is inherently vile and destructive, yet they did it anyway, one millen-
nium after another, something as close to
insane as any other description. But the
human Species was far from insane; their
sense of order and calculated behaviors
are often elegant and what we would call
magical.

Your bill is due, _____ said,
her eyes wet and salty, her hand a stone.

*So much to pay. Aren't I owed a last
request?*

*The Corporation would've given you
anything.*

Not this, not you, dear. That much I had to take.

A very, very long time ago a tiny man—tiny in comparison to his peers, who had larger shoulders and larger penises and more mates in awe of those large shoulders and genital girth—had an idea. The tiny man noticed that with large shoulders and large penises came more food and sex and an occasional murder to protect the food and sex and stave off the boredom that comes with the same food and sex. The tiny man noticed that the food and sex were not manifestations of the shoulders and penises—a shoulder and penis cannot make bread or meat—but they can persuade others to surrender them. And so his neurons fired and sprouted the wondrous idea of Persuasion. Humans could be persuaded with visual cues that represent things they desire, such as the strength to procure a meal out of fear of losing the strength to procure a meal. The penis situation generally needs no analysis.

Without the concept of Hoarding, Persuasion for the tiny man would've been useless. So he hoarded his food and used that to persuade larger men to protect it and surrender their mating options, and from that came princes and governments, towns, municipalities, and, of course, taxes. Certainly, there were wise occupants of those times who were bad at hoarding and recognized the unnecessary nature of owing another person anything, but they were murdered eventually or immediately and human beings paid taxes till the end of their days.

We mention taxes at length for the marvel, certainly, but also because the Nation sat atop the hierarchy of debts and debtors. Through obvious mechanisms of greed and gluttony, everyone owed the Nation, including _____ and Anemone.

Why the Grave?

Because you hate it here! Anemone laughed. *The sensations—damp, cold, heat, sewage. Isn't it terrible!*

Everything here is a failure, their gods and bodies. It's full of rotted everything.

Anemone blew air across her lips in mockery and amusement.

You're such a propagandist. It's frustrating. Sexy.

Anemone, please. You're going to die today.

At that breathless declaration, Anemone paused and smiled up at the sky's ambivalence.

I've been coming to the Grave since I was a teenager, dearest. They're so mis-

erable here and still delighted to exist and would have it no other way. I cannot calculate these kinds of people.

They are mummies, Anemone! Ancient dead things.

Propaganda! They are alive. They are us—well, without the perks of citizenship and the tech of marginal immortality. Let me show you . . . before I go.

Anemone walked around the barrel of _____'s weapon to put both hands on her face.

Here or there we are monsters and angels, Anemone said, *terrors too grotesque, too frightful to look at with bare eyes. Here is all that matters. Here they remember; they feel; they are alive like a wound, like birth, like a storm. What else could be more important? What else would keep me anywhere so long? For what else would I pay more than I have to give?*

FRIDAY

INSTEAD OF TELLING HER NIECE her father has died horribly or adhering to an essential evening routine of fastidious dental and skin care, Coral again took to the dating apps. Avoidance is a powerful drug. With her teeth unbrushed, Coral secured a date the next morning for tea that ended up being at an off-brand Long Beach no-kill shelter.

Coral never got good at drinking, which was the most common avoidance mechanism for adults going through periods of trauma that have no definitive end or recognizable beginning.

The Date had had her share of trauma, based on her slightly elevated tone of voice and sleepless eyes. She wore loose jeans with a cropped top that had a pair of life-size red lips stitched on the front; both were colorful and asymmetrical enough to have been acquired at a thrift store. The Date also had an eyebrow ring and a master's degree in library science, had eaten a banana-and-peanut-butter sandwich for breakfast, was probably low-needs autistic, which was difficult to diagnose in women, and had a Band-Aid on her index finger.

Coral had never been to the shelter in all her years of stomping around that city. It was lush on the outside and near the largest park in the area, one with multiple lakes and bridges that crossed major roads. She wished there was tea, though. Inside the shelter a different kind of longing took place. The animals, the cats and dogs of various ages and conditions, were a sad bunch of creatures. Coral could hear Sara McLachlan's "Angel" playing in her head from every ASPCA commercial. The cold, weary animals shivered in their concrete cages. When she first entered, Coral audibly gasped.

I know, said the Date. *At least they won't have to die here.*

Death would've been a gift. Coral said nothing.

The previous night, Coral calmed Khadija's increasingly panicked texts.

> Coral: I'll text him. Are you guys getting along right now?
>
> Coral: He said he's fine.
>
> Coral: Double shift.

Coral gasped because she was once afraid of dogs and took a long time before having one of her own. Plus she loved videos of animal attacks, which made her feel as though she had not missed out on something by not having a dog as a child. The videos left her vindicated and content in her bite-free skin and animal-free life.

When the Species discovered More, they had not planned on the wasteland of social media and online dating pools. More flourished in those spaces regardless of intent. The imaginary need to possess what cannot be quantified, what cannot be held in the palm, the fistful of water that is beauty, prestige, a life well lived, self-worth, a good sense of humor in a place designed to inflict pain, but call it being liked. There was always More online, producing a gluttonous vacuum of malcontents like a swarm of flies.

I need to tell you something, Coral said to the Date.

The urgent need to confess her sins, her truth, her reality came over Coral like a wave of diarrhea. She nearly grabbed the Date by the collar and shook her to make her see the gravity of the moment, but resisted when the stitching looked somewhat delicate and the tiny pair of lips embroidered on the shirt pocket became unbearable to behold.

There's one I want you to see, the Date replied, oblivious to Coral's emotional cresting.

Coral followed her in her now-fugue state through the corridors of horrifically depressed cats and dogs, like living wallpaper in a nightmare. She did not know all the breeds but tried to recognize some of them as a way of gaining power over the ordeal. She said the breed names aloud and kept her thoughts to herself. *Cocker spaniel*: one-eyed. *Mutt*: mange. *Pit bull*: dogfight loser. *Chihuahua*: loud and annoying. *Mutt*: fat. Coral then began complimenting the most unattractive dogs, the ones with missing patches of fur or missing or asymmetrical facial features due to birth defects, human error, or bad luck.

So sweet.

OMG. I love him.

What a champ.

In the Clinic for Outrageous Disguises That Cloak All Evidence of Frailty, Loneliness, and Terror, we have phobias. We do not conquer our phobias at appropriate moments. We are afraid of dogs and walk through shelters. The cages give us confidence, but we trust the cages only as much as we trust the people that have the keys and turn the locks. Those people seem like idiots. Fear is not a thing to conquer in one evening at a no-kill animal shelter with great marketing and poor actual maintenance. Fear is a thing to drown in other priorities.

Just as Coral's panic attack escalated to its pre-embarrassing crescendo, the Date pulled her into a larger cage they'd misnamed a greeting room, where Coral was met face-to-face with a cloud-white pit bull.

Her name is Carly. Why don't you hang out for a minute. I'm going to run to the restroom.

That's a good idea . . .

The cage door closed. Coral meant that the restroom was a good idea—being somewhere other than this place she found herself in was a good idea. There was no time for that to be communicated. The room had only a bench and a metal bowl of murky water, assumed to be for Carly. Carly was large and impeccable, no scarring from fights, just one blue eye and one hazel one in a large face, big as Coral's torso; her jowls closed fine, didn't hang like butcher meat the way some of the others did. Carly knew she was beautiful, and that it wouldn't save her.

Coral's panic attack continued.

In the Clinic for Dying While Willfully Participating in a Poorly Thought-Out Cultural Trend and Becoming a Martyr for Revolution, we confess our most recent horror to the nearest living thing, a creature of no consequence, in an act of delirium, dehydration, nausea, and undiagnosed psychosis. The creature is a dog. She responds to our confession like a dog would, with a tilted head and periodic licking of her paws and genitals.

At the climax of her panic attack, Coral passed out

alone on the concrete bench with a large adult pit bull in the so-called greeting room, unattended. If Carly had been a different animal, Coral would've been in trouble. Showing weakness to animals is not always met with kindness. Other creatures like chimps or hogs might've chewed her face off. Carly was more indifferent than kind, but Coral was all the better for it.

Within a few moments, the Date and other staff of the shelter entered in a fuss to check on Coral's overall life.

The EMT is on the way. I am so sorry. Are you okay?

Are you okay?

Are you on medications?

Did I pass all the way the fuck out?

Yes! they all replied.

I am so sorry. I sometimes watch people I meet through the glass to see how they interact with Carly. She doesn't live here. She's mine, and I bring her as a kind of therapy dog for the other dogs. They don't always get along but mostly they get along, and it's nice for Carly to get out and see what the world is, you know.

No. I don't know.

I heard what you said in here too. I'm so sorry about your brother.

Coral stood up and left the room, a little wobbly but with most of her dignity. Then she doubled back to get the bottle of water the staff had brought for her, and then left the building without a word and drove away.

We stand in agreement with Coral. Fuck that. The morning was still bright and more humid than Coral would've liked. She blamed the lush park for the temperature of the air and would get a coffee as a reward for all she had just experienced. Before More there was Just

Enough and after More there was Less, an emptying-out of desire and possessions in hopes of acquiring something intangible as a replacement. More never went away. In the exhaustion of avoidance and the cold blast of air from her car's AC, Coral thought only of revenge, revenge against the Date, against Carly, against the no-kill fucking shelter, against the dating apps, against Jay and his immunity to it all, against Khadija and her need, her vanity, her naivete, and still Coral felt unsatisfied. She had all the rage and not much time.

In the coffee shop's drive-thru line, Coral is visited by four ghosts. This particular drive-thru was not well designed, because it was originally a residential street converted into a strip mall with parking spots designed for tiny 1980s Toyotas. Somehow people made things work across the decades where car sizes swelled and slowly carved their mammoth vehicles along the tight space around the building to the pickup window. Coral could not smell the ocean or hear it. She could see the bend of the earth toward the sea beyond the buildings, the concavity of the ground and the rise of water. She heard a woman scream *Fuck you* to an invisible man at the light-rail station. Many people had their ghosts come to them that morning.

Coral's first visitor was her mother. She opened the door and sat in the back seat, and like anyone familiar with that part of the world, Coral thought she was about to fight or die. Then she recognized the woman, who had not aged in the sixteen years since Coral had learned of her death, rattling in costume jewelry, extensions firm and scratching against the leather.

I don't need your help.

Her mother twitched her mouth as if about to speak and then adjusted the collar of her outdated blazer, heavy on the shoulder pads.

In the Clinic for Excavating Repressed Memories in Search of Solutions to Current Crises, we walk through novelty corn mazes during the month of October in search of fear. We do not scare easily and never have but we love to watch those that do. We are cannibals. We are numb. We believe we have suffered losses more real and incalculable than any monster imagined could deliver.

Coral looked at her own face in her rearview mirror and realized she was older than her mother then. Her mother leaned forward and looked as though she were about to gossip about something juicy, something about a neighbor or the Aunts, and Coral remembered a woman full of language and stories and lies that she'd not really thought about much at all. Coral leaned back to hear, hungry for scandal, and was alone.

The concept of More did not exist only for inanimate objects or the bodies of people as in more wine, more sex. More applied to time with people as well when the idea of goodbye could not properly be established for various reasons. When children are taken forever or die, parents want More, more birthdays and lunches and shopping and phone calls about plans to go on vacation and get braces and join sports teams with insufferable other parents and family medical insurance and college scholarships and marijuana.

When friends die before a proper goodbye, people want More too. They want more adventures and alcohol and crimes of various proportions and sugar and safety and the feeling that there is no clock between them, because they were born around the same time and can die around that time, so there is no need to ever grieve for very long.

The line of cars had moved along some when her next ghost sat in the passenger seat. He had a hard time sliding down into the sports car, his large frame groaning the entire way, exhaling hard as his knees pressed into the dashboard.

The car's cute, though, Coral said, rubbing her steering wheel.

Her father laughed, all smoke and leather.

Practical is boring. You always said to get what you really want. Settling is for losers or something. I don't think you said "losers." It's a rough paraphrase, you know. Something happened, Daddy, and I don't know what to do.

Coral's throat seized up and it was nearly time for her to place her order. This was no place to have a sudden and deeply warranted emotional breakdown. Baristas have enough to manage without the labor of consoling troubled women.

Coral put both hands on her knees and spread the fingers out wide. Her father, next to her, had already done the same, his fingers a shade darker and much larger.

You need to cut your nails, Daddy.

It was time to place her order. The blue SUV ahead of her drove around the tight corner and out of sight. Coral was speaking out of her window when the passenger door opened and closed. The weight in the vehicle shifted. The leather and smoke were replaced with hairspray and strawberries and cream body lotion. Coral continued her order from habit, from memory, her heart a fireworks show behind the bones and her hoodie. She finished the order turned to her right and said, *I'm sorry.*

There was Naima, full of light, a teenager in Nike Cortezes with the pink swoosh and gold hoops, demure, shy, and at the place she'd worked hard to be in, pretending she only happened to arrive by chance. Naima began to take off her jewelry, then her shoes, then her top and shorts.

What is happening?

Naima didn't stop undressing in the car, dropping the earrings and clothing out the window, until she was there, naked. Her breasts were low and she had the folds and markings of a mother, striations of living around her navel and areolas. Coral stared at safe places for a few seconds, the radio volume dial, Naima's knees, and the wrist bone that protruded like a defect but was perfectly normal.

Coral then looked straight ahead into the empty stretch of drive-thru lane and took off her hoodie. She pulled her T-shirt over her head, unfastened her bra, and pushed the mass of clothing into her lap. Her body had not delivered any children into this world, but gravity had done its work to pull and stretch regardless.

When she bent down to undo her shoelaces there was a struggle. Her car was not designed to be a dressing room, and when she sat upright, finally having removed her left shoe, there sat Jay next to her.

Goddamn it, Jay! What the fuck, dude?

Coral covered her breasts and put her T-shirt back on as the car behind her gently honked for her to drive forward. She didn't have time to bother with her bra as her own car beeped at her continuously for not wearing her seat belt.

Goddamn it! So what nightmare do you have for me? The others weren't so bad. The last one got a little weird.

Coral put her head into her hand out of exhaustion and embarrassment. She laughed a little through wet eyes.

It's not fucking funny, you asshole.

She finally looked over at her brother, a teenager, a lightweight, white T-shirt and blue jeans, too tall to be comfortable in the car but thin enough not to be bothered. He held a Discman with metal headphones corded to it. After a couple of seconds he took the CD out of the Discman and tried to slide it into the car player. He smelled of the ocean and fish and had no shoes on. There was sunlight hot on his head and face, as if he were outdoors on a boat.

I love this fucking song.

Jay turned it up. They both sat there in T-shirts growing damp from ocean spray, listening to Snoop Dogg.

When Coral arrived at the pickup window, the attendant handed her five drinks, four of them in a caddy. She had no time to protest, but paid and accepted the order she didn't remember placing. Coral put the drinks on the empty seat next to her, along with her shoe and hoodie and bra.

In the Clinic for Telling Lies to Avoid Pending Death, we say we've been here before. We say that each new loss, each new goodbye, teaches us how to handle the next one and the one after that. We say many things that are not really true. We do not say that each death is different, each goodbye will rip in new and unforeseeable ways, and the pain is never exactly the same. We do not say that there is grace in communing with the dead and each will surprise you from memory to imagination, the ways their shapes become our shapes over time or right away. We do not say that you will order coffee for the dead and there are things we will never forget about the ghosts that visit us, our murdered and our friends.

In an inexplicable move of honesty and adulthood, Coral decided to initiate contact with Khadija.

Coral: Are you at the apartment?

Coral already knew the answer. She asked as herself, through her own phone, in her own words, which were easier to access than anything she'd ever said before.

Khadija: Yes.

Coral: I'm on my way.

Khadija: Ok.

In the Clinic for Telling Lies to Avoid Pending Death, we study goodbye. We say goodbye to our enemies, to history books and lovers, as if it is the end and we will not rehearse every failure, every triumph, all the little ways we misunderstand love and death, over again the next day and the next life as the orphans of a Species that almost had it all.

One thing we practice on occasion, but less often than making love in nearly empty movie theaters and bingeing on chocolate cupcakes for the serotonin high, is sleep. We know the metaphorical link between sleep and death is an obvious footnote in the indices of humanity and how collectively they went to sleep when all their problems got really, really hard. They stopped thinking in the same reality and retreated to separate ones, losing consciousness and dreaming in lies, like accidentally destroying your own nation with a biological weapon meant for a neighbor, an easy mistake.

When Coral had her face licked by an eighty-pound pit bull named Carly, met her brother's ghost, and drove to his home, she glimpsed the unnamable thing. We speculate that it is spore related, earth related, family related, water related, the invisible tendrils that connect all living things so they are never truly alone.

The coffees were still fresh as Coral searched for a parking spot at the apartment, two iced and three hot. She decided it was best to take them all, holding her own in one hand as she carried the others in the caddy. On the sidewalk, she passed by many patches of dried animal poop and weeds sprouting through the cracks in the ground.

Perhaps Coral was less of a killer and more of a hoarder after all. She wanted more just like all of her Species wanted More. She wanted more chances to do better and a little time just to live unrestricted, as many used to wish for. Women her age wanted more youth and money and were stupid for the trouble. We know this as law. Coral wanted Khadija to have more too. Still, Coral was a non-mother, and non-mothers were not often trusted with things that had to do with babies or tax credits or authority over strollers and their reproductive itineraries in many states for a time. Coral had had no authority over Khadija ever, really, and was just an Aunt. She knew she would fuse one day into the Aunts, a younger, more stylish limb of the hive, offering good advice quietly over brunch and then fading like a cloud on a hot day.

Coral could feel her heart stuttering in the manner of fear. Khadija terrified her. The future was terrifying. Coral feared imposing trauma where there was none before, and as much as Coral, like us, could destroy her enemies and rest well, she had a rule about never causing pain to those on whom we practiced love. Because she was an artist and a creator of dramatic worlds, Coral understood bad choices, how to engage with them like magic tricks, allow them their time to dazzle and enthrall before they must be wrangled back into a hat like bunnies and doves, to wait for other audiences.

In the Clinic for Dying While Willfully Participating in a Poorly Thought-Out Cultural Trend and Becoming a Martyr for Revolution, we are at Universal Studios Hollywood for the many-dozenth time with our brother and niece. They are thirty and twelve. They are twenty-three and five. Our brother eats a hot dog like a boy, fast and messy, as the clouds change the light from harsh to gray, from gold to soft. We watch a couple steal hats from the souvenir shop by just putting them on and walking out, and this makes us ashamed and we don't know why. We believe in this memory like we believe in bacon on Saturday mornings and Christmas trees until New Year's Day. That is how happiness works; it is faith and forgetting that there is so much else to worry about. When we are there again our niece is twenty. We see the crowds and remember different ones. There are ice cream and mist machines and boys vomiting into trash cans and weak novelty cocktails. This time it is exhausting and whenever we cry we look away from each other and know that we will never come back here again, because here is not there anymore. We know one day we will remember him in that place without pain, like reading a street sign with a familiar name in a new city. Then we will be able to smile because the sign is so far away and passes behind us as long as we keep going forward. We say goodbye.

Coral approaches the gate to the apartment building and thinks Khadija might handle this well. There is a resolve in her that comes with growing up where she did, in the body that she had—often described as strength, but really a kind of desensitization to trauma. *This might hurt less to her than someone else*, Coral thought.

Fuck.

Yes, because it was true, and also yes, because it did not have to be true. And then again, Coral remembered a sensitive girl that trained herself to manage deprivation under the promise that More could come Later with a little patience and hard work. Coral did not have a speech prepared for such stratospheric levels of bullshit. Then Coral wondered if this was how Khadija would become her own mother, and if Coral had ever become *her* own mother, just with more money. They were both averse to being responsible for anyone other than themselves. Because Coral was often a grown-up, she did not blame her mother for anything, also because that would involve crediting her mother for some things as well, which was not an option.

Coral passed through the front gate with all the coffees, now more watery and changed under the heat of the walk over and the settling of their syrups and sugars to less optimal locations in the cups.

The courtyard, as it was officially called, had not changed much over the week. All the children were away and most adults had left as well, except for the wives that were always home and always watching. The bougainvillea sparkled and the gardenias needed watering, their leaves rimmed in brown. From a distance Coral could see some of the shrines outside unit #5, the candle with the Virgin of Guadalupe on the front and the Santeria monument of unidentifiable bits of metal and vegetation, which Coral dared not discard as often as she had every other note of condolence left that week by neighbors. From a distance, Coral could also see that the door to #5 was open and the darkness within was exposed to the air of the day. Khadija stepped out of the apartment into the light, unable to wait for Coral to actually make it all the way up there before laying eyes on her.

Coral looked away, away at the brick fencing between the complex and the neighboring duplex. She'd called the police for domestic violence against those neighbors years ago. She remembered their cries. A television laugh track played from the apartment on the bottom floor just then as Coral approached the stairs with all her coffees, unable to hold on to the railing as she ascended. She eventually looked up to see that Khadija had moved onto the stairs and looked down on Coral with her serious brow furrowed, and then the change, whatever part Coral had to play, required no words and was finished as soon as Khadija saw her face. The worry changed to knowing as if all Coral's ghosts ushered her forward, and every screeching thing went silent under the scream.

In the minutes to follow all the coffees went bad, missed their chance, never really had one.

Upon graduation we are reminded that endings are absolute in some ways but not in all. Tomorrow we belong to the unnamable thing, which requires only that we try. What quakes and burns in the cosmos will always roar with or without warning. We must bear the sound.

Acknowledgments

The shape of mourning is varied. This book is just one size but not all. I try not to count my losses too often, but I have learned that not everyone we love can always stay with us as long as we'd like. I'm grateful to those whom I love and who have loved me back for a minute to whenever the clock stopped for us. To my oldest friends, Pam and Deneta, thank you for keeping me and for your unwavering, unconditional friendship. Thanks to my agent, the mighty Jin Auh, and my editor, Jackson Howard, for your precision and sincerity. Also, thanks to Emily Bell, wherever you are, for acquiring this work when it was just a whispered idea.

Always a special thanks to my Fresno fam, Ginny, Brynn, and Araceli. You are graceful and funny and generous, and I'm lucky to know you. Butterbean is lucky to know you too. I love you all.

To my brothers, Donald and Derek, thanks for sharing and guarding our memory of life in the Blackburn household. I love you. To all my nieces and nephews, I apologize for any accidental damage brought on by watching me live. To my aunts Susie Green and Venissa Horrington, thank you for looking out for me all these years when your sister couldn't. I love and appreciate you in all the words. To my mother, to whom I attribute all my gifts, I miss you.

Venita Blackburn is the author of the story collections *Black Jesus and Other Superheroes*, which won the Prairie Schooner Book Prize and was a finalist for the New York Public Library Young Lions Fiction Award and the PEN/Robert W. Bingham Prize for Debut Short Story Collection, and *How to Wrestle a Girl*, which was a finalist for the Lambda Literary Award for Lesbian Fiction and the Ernest J. Gaines Award for Literary Excellence. Her stories have appeared in *The New Yorker* online, *The Paris Review*, *Pleiades*, *Bat City Review*, and *American Short Fiction*. She is an associate professor in the creative writing program at California State University, Fresno, and is the founder and president of Live, Write, an organization that offers free creative writing workshops for communities of color. She lives in Fresno.